INNOCENCE IN THE SHADOWS

Joanny Donnelly

Contents

Prologue

"Chief, come quickly. I hear some shuffles from this side of the forest."

"I do, too. Let's go."

Pushing past the thick forest branches, the Embalian Police squad rushed across the forest floor and the sticky puddles irritating their souls. The air was moist and wet, and it was the sound of the buzzings mixed with the smell of blood that made many feel sick with nausea.

Stomping across the fallen leaves, the chief of the police pushed a huge bush aside and immediately ordered his force to halt as he eyed a young man lying in the middle of an open meadow. The man seemed to be brutally clawed by an animal with his hands frozen in a manner that showed he had been trying to defend himself. Next to him was a young woman sitting perfectly fine. She was curled up into a ball and crying her heart out.

"Miss!" The chief ran towards her with a blanket, while the rest of the task force rushed towards the man.

This was one of the first Embalia killings.

The girl, who had been sitting next to the young man, would be present in all the other crime scenes, usually crying her heart out. She carried no weapons, no tools, except for a baseball bat, and the clawed victims were free of any finger marks.

It was one of the most blogging cases that required the best detective in Asia to intervene and solve the case.

CHAPTER 1

Z ayan

Taking slow sips of black coffee, Detective Zayan sat in his office with a black hat tilted and lazily resting on his thick messy locks, his feet casually resting against the edge of a small coffee table and his head leaned against the headrest of the armchair. There was only a single yellow lamp resting on his table.

It was just this afternoon when the Embalian police had sent him the case file and an audio recording of one of the deadliest killing sprees occurring in the forest of Embalia. Zayan didn't usually take a lot of cases because he found most of them boring, yet this case had intrigued him; especially when the murders committed seemed simply a case of animal attacks but consisted of one common eye-witness: Miss Nyla Khawar-the woman he had got married to last year and then left with the intention of divorcing her. She was some far-away family friend's daughter, had been his grandfather's choice. Not his. He didn't even know her, never spared her another thought, until he had heard that she was being pursued by the police.

He had been irritated that some unstable criminal was his grandfather pick for him. He knew that he was in no position to get offended by such a match, had demons of his own, but it had felt like his family no longer bothered about him. They had been bent on punishing him for all that he had done by trapping him in a business-like marriage. His irritation had then turned into morbid fascination. He wanted to bring his wife to justice. His grandfather had been begging him not to divorce her, to get to know her first.

However, upon turning on the audio, Zayan's heartbeat stopped a little upon hearing Nyla speak in a tiny voice. She seemed to have such a sweet and innocent aura, catching him completely off guard. This was the woman who was being suspected of murder, the woman he was thinking of divorcing?

He had been a darn fool.

Charmed, shocked and captivated, he kept listening in an awestruck manner while feeling his heartbeat grow wild. Wow! This was insanity, He felt guilty of being fascinated by her, knowing beauty never equated innocence, yet he knew that this intrigue and infatuation would keep him more invested and dedicated in order to find the truth.

Mesmerized, Zayan knew that this world was full of beautiful facades. He didn't want to be fooled by another. Especially when the last one had caused him to spend five years in jail.

Feeling intrigued, he then started studying Nyla's profile.

Name: Nyla Khawar

Age: 24

Status: single

Ethnicity: born and raised in Embalia

Occupation: a struggling columnist

Background: when little, Nyla would often be taken to psychiatrists by her parents. Her medical details show that she used to claim that she would see some strange humans at night time. She was later diagnosed as struggling with an extreme case of schizophrenia, depression and anxiety. However, the symptoms of these issues started to diminish as she grew older. In fact, in 2005, she was declared healthy by her doctors, suffering from only a mild form of depression. (All of her medical reports have been attached with this file).

Family: she belongs to a middle-class family. Her father is a local shop manager while her mother is a housewife. Both of her parents are loving and kind. They show no signs of any irregularities and are adored by their community. Neighbours say that the Khawar family are the friendliest folks in town.

Her parents have also been called in for questioning, and they claim that Nyla is a sweet, kind and gentle girl who can never hurt a fly. She is fragile and easily gets overwhelmed.

Her childhood problems still have a huge impact on her personality, but she is not the one who can harm a soul.

Friends: Miss Nyla reportedly doesn't have any close friends. She used to tutor her neighbour kids and is on friendly terms with their mothers, but she lives with her parents and only leaves her house for either grocery shopping, visiting her relatives' houses and going for night walks around 9 to 10 pm at a forest located a street away from her house. Also, she is married, but her husband's information is unavailable. They have separated

She works from home, and her former college classmates have recognized her to be one of those quiet, sensitive and rather fragile girls who used to sit alone near the trash cans during the breaks and was an easy target for bullies and aggressive teachers. Sources have claimed that she never fought back, never spoke a word to anyone or complained to the admin staff about the bullying. She took it all with a weak smile.

She studied at Kiran College for Women

Current Case: Miss Nyla Khawar was found crying on the crime scene of the 'Embalia Forest' Killings. She seemed completely fine-unharmed and safe, while she sat next to the victims that seemed to be preyed upon by animals. Some pictures of the claw marks found on the crime scene have been attached as evidence.

(THIS IS HOW ONE OF THE VICTIMS' CAR WAS FOUND PARKED OUTSIDE THE FOREST)

Fully engrossed in the case file, Zayan spent the rest of the night studying profiles of the case victims and chewing on his thumbnails. The warmth of his coffee was not enough to keep up with his mind's pace.

The next morning

Grabbing a coffee cup from the break room, Zayan held the case file under his arm and walked towards the interrogation room. The police had already informed him that all the female detectives had failed to make the suspect crack, and now it was solely up to him to make Nyla confess. He was going to investigate such a sweet criminal.

A smirk appeared on his face as he momentarily stood outside the room, staring at Nyla from the room's one-way mirror window. His wife was fidgeting, nervously looking around, sighing and just too beautiful.

He was in love.

Shaking his head in amusement at such a surprising epiphany while wondering how she would react upon seeing him, given he knew that she too considered their marriage as a business, he then pushed open the door and stepped inside. It was time to interrogate one of the sweetest and surprising suspects. Her doe eyes sharply turned towards him as he stepped into the room. He noticed her tiny gasp echo in the air and caught it with a grin.

What a charming surprise!

No way was he going to let her go now.

"Ma'am Nyla Khawar. I am Detective Zayan from the Asian task force. I have been appointed to deal with your case. I will just like to ask a few questions from you today. Is that fine?" He sat across from her. There was an interrogation table between them. He was keeping things professional. He didn't want the cameras to catch that he knew Nyla. It would lead to unnecessarily questioning he felt too bored to answer.

"Sure." She half-shrugged, catching the drift, already looking so small as she avoided his gaze. Her gesture seemed shy, cute, awkward and enough to make a man want to tip her chin up and witness her smile.

This woman was his wife. Wow!

She knew just how to make a man fall.

He had been missing out--big time.

"Hmm, Nyla," he then stood up and started pacing across the floor. "You have been found to be present on the crime scene of the Embalia Killings case. You have been seen to be present at the crime scenes crying your heart out. Can you give me an exact detail of what exactly you saw at those crime scenes?" He momentarily turned his head towards her.

"Umm...sure." She obediently nodded, keeping her gaze fixated on the surface of the table. "I was having my night-time walks-"

"In the forest?" He interrupted with a curious look.

"Y-yes, I enjoy visiting the forest lake at night," she quickly defended, briefly meeting his gaze. This was her side of the world, the story he had never before bothered with.

Pinching his chin, he then gestured her to continue as he listened with his hands folded behind his back.

"Umm...so I was out for a forest walk when I heard someone screaming in pain."

"Are you telling me about the first person who got killed?" He stopped her again.

"Umm...y-yes," she reluctantly spoke, nervously touching her eyebrows. She seemed too cautious or, perhaps, too guilty. Yet there was such an innocent aura around her.

So cute.

"Okay, so you were all alone and you heard a man scream-ing in pain, so you ran towards him. Am I right?" he then summarized, coming to stand behind the chair he had been sitting on, his gaze on her.

She nodded. "That is true. I heard him yelling for help and immediately rushed towards him, but he had already been attacked and left bleeding on the forest floor by some animal," she explained, sounding remorseful. Like the killings had saddened her.

Interesting.

Zayan ran his right hand through his heavy locks. He was now suppressing a smirk from appearing on his face as he raised one eyebrow at Nyla, his hands fisting into the leather back of the chair. "So, Nyla, what I am understanding is that you like to take night walks in the forest with no weapons-"

"No, I carry my father's baseball bat around." She quickly shook her head.

"Yes, of course," he gave her a dashing smile. "You go for night-time walks around 9 to 10 pm, carry only a baseball bat for protection and witness people mauled by animals. Is that alright?"

"Mr Zayan," she fumed, grabbing the side of the table in anger.

"You can simply call me Zayan. You have the right to do so," he charmed with a knowing look, making the woman huff with indignation.

"Mr Zayan," she spoke through gritted teeth, completely ignored his comment, making him suppress an amused smile. She was feigning complete ignorance. "The forest is my second home. I have been going for my night time walks since I was a little girl. It might be strange for you to believe since you don't know me, yet the animals of that forest don't harm me. They are familiar with me so don't treat me as an outsider," she scowled. She honestly looked quite insulted by the accusation, like she wanted to show a naive side. She seemed to really hate his guts. Understandable.

Her words sounded so strange.

Everyone knows that wild animals spare no one. She wanted to make many believe that she didn't believe in that fact.

What an odd thing to do.

"Hmm, but why is it that the forest Killings occur when you are out for a walk? And why do you go back each time? I mean witnessing someone clawed by an animal must be a traumatizing sight for women." He feigned an innocent look as he folded his arms and eyed her.

She winced for a second and then lowered her head in defeat. "I-It is. I h-haven't been able to sleep for ages, but I need my nighttime walks. They help me forget somethings...soothe my depression away-y." she tried explaining. She sounded so weak and miserable.

He knew what she was talking about.

"Are those things perhaps your childhood memories?" He inquired knowingly, ignoring how his heart hurt at her expressions. She didn't respond.

"Nyla, has anyone told you that you have pretty eyes?" He then mused thoughtfully, making her look up in confusion and slight anger.

"Umm...no?" She gave him a questioning look, hiding some irritation.

"That is a shame." He spoke under his breath.

"Excuse me-"

"Has one of the boys at your college have ever approached you?" He continued.

"I beg your pardon-"

"Have they?" He persisted, making her sigh and then shake her head, lowering her gaze back towards the table. He wanted to make sure that his absence hadn't earned her any admirers. The jealousy was real.

Now that he had met her, he was willing to stake his claim.

"No. I studied in an all-girls college. Also, men don't usually go for women with a medical record," Her voice drifted into a tiny and depressed mood again.

The thought of so many boys missing out on marrying this woman deeply thrilled Zayan because he knew that he was the lucky man who was going to get keep her.

Sweet.

"They are honest fools." He sat before her again and then cupped his chin while facing her. She obviously looked so uncomfortable and confused by his behaviour. She pushed her chair slightly away from the table as she tried avoiding his gaze and kept her eyes fixated on her hands.

"You used to be picked on a lot in college, right?" he continued, ignoring her fidgeting stance.

"Umm...yes," she softly spoke, a sense of shame heavy in her voice.

"Did that ever make you rage?" He frowned.

"Yes." She quietly accepted. It seemed like this was a hard topic for her to talk about.

"But why didn't you retaliate?" He tilted his head. He was curious.

What was this woman thinking?

"I-I didn't know how." She sounded so broken...so forlorn. His heart squeezed in sympathy.

"Hmm...but now you do, right?" He stood up again and went back to pacing around the room. "Some of the victims found in the forests are your former classmates and former colleagues. Many of them wronged you, and now you are old enough to fight back. Killing them in the forest makes them pay for what they did to you."

"I didn't do it!" She stood up, too, in rage, her voice determined and high-pitched. "I don't know what exactly is happening, but, Mr Zayan, you are asking the wrong person for some answers. In fact, I know my rights, and I know that I don't even have to answer your questions, but I am only here because I want to help the victim's families in becoming settled with the truth."

"You know I spend five years in jail trying to cover up someone else's lies." He stayed calm as he dealt with her anger. "If there is some gang behind you, something you are hiding from us, tell me now. I can guarantee that we will go easy on you. I will go easy on you." He moved closer, leaning on the table.

Her shoulders slumped again. "I am telling you that I didn't do anything." There was a desperate plea like she wanted anyone to believe her truth. She seemed so lost.

"Okay," he gave in, pinching the bridge of his nose, knowing he owed her this after everything. "But we will have to keep you in our police cell for some days. Just as a caution. Will you allow us to do that?" he gently spoke, offering a smile, as he fought the urge to caress her cheek.

She sighed and then nodded, wrapping her arms around herself. "Yes, of course. Anything to help the police. But I have just one favour to ask."

"What?" He frowned...his eyebrows narrowed in curiosity.

"I want a white light to be lit at all times in my cell. Also, I want to share my cell with another female prisoner."

What an odd request.

Nyla

With the midnight clock slowly ticking, I sat on the bench of the prison cell while having my hands tightly gripping its edge. Long locks of my hair were fallen free, my neck was bent towards the floor, and my cellmate was sleeping on the bench opposite from me.

Soon the clock struck one, I eyed the dark hallway outside my cell and gulped. They were here. With their heads (sideways and poking up from behind the walls of the hallway) illuminated by my cell lights, expressionless eyes wide open and huge blank grins, they were peaking inside my cell, staring straight at me.

Chapter 2

Zayan

Wearing his black ray-bans, Zayan tapped on the steering wheeling and easily reversed his red Lamborghini into the Kiran College for Women's parking lot. There were young females eyeing his car with impressed looks...a sudden interest had started echoing in the air. Sheriff Bahadur (a partner assigned to him by the police) was sitting next to him, on the passenger seat, holding on to the seat in fear.

Peering at him from over his glasses in amusement, Zayan suppressed a smirk and finally parked his car. He was a speed junkie. He never went slow, and, apparently, his craze for thrill had turned Sheriff Bahadur completely white.

Chuckling at his partner's small heart, he got out of the car, earning subtle sighs from around, and then hung his glasses from his collar. The Kiran College for Women, one of his old colleagues used to like a girl from this college. She simply brother-zoned him and had that poor man attend her wedding.

Women.

Shaking his head, he had his partner join him outside and then began heading towards the secured entrance of the college. The weather was blazing hot, with the sunlight reflecting off his glasses. Ignoring the gazes from all corners, he showed his card at the entrance and rolled his eyes as one of the security men, insecure by all the attention he was receiving, tried to act manly and started asking him some absurd questions. A simple show of the Sheriff's badge was quick to mellow down his macho-attitude.

Soon, after being allowed inside the college, he eyed its huge gardens, in-door parking area and peered up at its old towering buildings with curiosity. This college had just turned a hundred years old. Its PG-Post Graduate block...that is where he had to go right now...that is where the office of the college's headmaster was situated.

Sherrif Bahadur looked so irritated by the huge number of fangirls Zayan had suddenly gained at this place, but Zayan was used to this behaviour. This was why he had once fallen for a woman who pretended to show no interest in him. That confusion and vainness...it had cost him so many years of his life, the reason why he never really gave his marriage a chance.

Smirking as a group of girls stood giggling nearby, he headed towards the PG block and smiled at the sight of so many females making way for him. Such delicate females...they were just so tender-hearted.

The headmaster 'Bashir Khan' had a whole waiting area for the guests. There was a reception area there, and Zayan could only roll his eyes at the sight of an elderly woman (around the age of his mother) who was sitting at the reception desk, turn cliche sweet while informing him to wait. This much attention was so annoying, sometimes.

Soon, he-only he-was allowed to go and meet Bashir Khan.

Bashir Khan's office had its walls covered by photo frames and old clippings of newspapers. There were files piled up upon the office sofas and a clean desk that had a small globe placed in one corner. Somehow, this scene was teasing Zayan's OCD tendencies.

Sher Khan, himself, was talking on the phone while sitting behind his desk. Upon seeing Zayan, he gestured him to sit and quickly ended the call.

"It is a pleasure to meet you," He shook Zayan's hand.

"Same." Zayan could only offer him a polite smile.

Sitting on the chair, that was placed on the other side of the desk, opposite Bashir Khan, Zayan leaned back and ruffled his hair.

"Tea?" Bashir Khan offered, picking up the phone.

"Coffee..." This was to show who was really leading this meeting.

Soon, after moments of making small talks, Zayan decided to get to the main point...he had been observing. The Headmaster looked like a man who cared a lot about his image. He had a small family; a wife who worked as an interior designer, two children: a girl and a boy, and a tamed lion. This man reflected society's version of success.

"Bashir Khan," Zayan didn't bother with the formalities. "As you know, one of your former students has been accused of committing heinous crimes-"

"Yes, Miss Nyla Khawar," Bashir Khan quickly interrupted in a rather patronizing tone, relaxing against his armchair, as if he didn't enjoy having his college being associated with the gentle and sweet Nyla.

Zayan's eyebrows narrowed. "You seem irritated." He observed, biting on his thumbnail.

"I just don't enjoy my college brought into the limelight for all the wrong reasons." The Headmaster was firm. He pulled out a file from under his desk and pushed it before Zayan. "I had my assistant pull out her file. Apparently, she was an average student, got mediocre grades, and only once took part in some annual scriptwriting competition. She wasn't visible enough in this college."

"She was visible enough to get pushed around by some college bullies," Zayan pointed, leaning back against his chair with a knowing look. The office door opened and, soon, two hot mugs of coffee were placed before him.

Ah, the medicine for his mind.

He almost had the urge of placing his feet up on the desk and sipping on his mug of coffee, yet he knew that this wasn't the place to relax-especially when he needed some answers. Maybe later. Inhaling the steam of his coffee, he cupped the coffee mug and closed his eyes. Bashir Khan almost looked weirded out by this behaviour.

"So," he finally looked up, leaning towards the desk, "You have a lot of pictures in this office. What is that picture about?" He randomly pointed at the picture of a bandaged arm signed by many.

"Ah," Bashir Khan leaned back in his armchair and folded his arms, a rather nostalgic expression on his face. "My daughter was a wild toddler. Her terrible twos..." A low chuckle escaped, as he rolled his sleeves and showed Zayan the scars. "These are a result of her breaking a plate."

However, instead of finding the story morbidly amusing, Zayan could only stare at the scars in bewilderment. They...they looked like claw marks. Three long claw marks.

"Are you sure it was your daughter?" He quickly met his gaze.

Bashir Khan nodded with a proud smile. "I was feeding my princess when this happened."

"Hmm..." Placing the coffee cup back on the table, Zayan pinched his chin in thought. "Will you mind having you and your staff fill some forms for me? I would like to have some insight information about what are the teachers' reviews about Nyla Khawar. Also, make sure everyone writes their names on the form provided to you by my partner, Bahadur..."

"Sure." The Headmistress nodded, folding his hands and placing them on the desk.

"Oh, and one more thing," he spoke, standing up and picking up Nyla's academic file...a mischievous smirk was appearing on his face. "You forgot to add that Nyla has hauntingly beautiful eyes. She can really destroy a man's heart with one gaze." The Headmaster looked so confused by this.

Chuckling, Zayan headed out of the office.

"Sir, how did it go?"

"Good." Zayan vaguely nodded.

"So what did the Headmaster say?"

"He forgot to mention that Nyla has beautiful eyes," He smirked, eyeing the confused expressions of his partner.

"Sir-" However, before Bahadur could speak, Zayan halted and stared at a group of boys gathered around a white Pajero. The girls' college building was situated right next to the boys' college, and the students of both colleges got to share the same parking light.

Emir Junaid-the brother of one of the girls killed-was sitting on the Pajero's hood and had a bunch of jocks surrounding them.

"They seem immature." He pointed with a raised eyebrow, unamused. Bahadur stared in the direction he was staring at.

"Nadia's brother!" Bahadur connected the dots. "Let's ask questions from him, too. We have the complete profiles of the victims' cases, yet maybe, you can get some insights."

A chance to berate a jock who might be around Nyla's age? Heck yeah!

Smiling, Zayan headed towards the jocks' group. Casually, he pulled off Bahadur's badge, making the man scoff, and attached the badge with his collar. The heat was growing intense now. The parking lot was nearly empty with a few ladies subtly walking by his Lamborghini.

Upon reaching the group, he carefreely pushed back one boy and showed his badge as the group stood up in anger.

"I need to have a word with Emir." He kept his gaze firm on the jock wearing so many chains, had his sleeves suffocatingly tight around his wrist. The boy's fashion sense seemed so opposite to the fashion sense of his peers, yet he seemed like one of those alpha men who led groups.

"The police, oh, busted..." One of the boys subtly nudged Emir, yet the jock seemed too nervous to laugh along.

"It's about your sister," Zayan added to quell the poor boy's heat. Visibly, he saw Emir's shoulder slump in relief.

"Sure."

"Okay, let's talk about it over a cup of coffee. You can lead me to your cafeteria."

"My sister wanted to collect some plants for her botany class. It was late, but she said she wanted to go."

"Why did you not go with her?" Zayan frowned, sipping on a cup of coffee that was given for free to him by the generous lunch lady. She had even added some extra spoons of everyday milk. Bahadur was attentively sitting next to him and taking notes, focusing completely on the words of Emir who was sitting on the opposite side of the table.

"I don't know." Emir shook his head, sounding thoroughly upset and confused about why he didn't join his sister for a late-night walk.

"Meaning?" He raised an eyebrow. The air-conditioner was situated right above his head, making him shiver. He didn't like feeling cold.

"I just don't remember why I didn't go with Nadia. We were like best friends. I-I can't really recall what made me let her go alone."

"Hmm..." He pinched his chin in thought, leaning back against his chair.

Bahadur chose to take over now. "What do you mean you don't remember? Your sister went alone at night, and you just let her go. What kind of careless attitude-

"Silence," he quickly spoke, sounding firm and serious.

"Emir," He turned towards the poor depressed boy. "Was your sister friendly with her classmate Nyla?"

"Umm...Nadia did, sometimes, joke about Nyla's shy and introverted ways," he confessed, scratching the back of his neck, looking away in guilt. Obviously, there was more to her just joking around. "But, I had seen that girl once in a supermart. She seemed sweet. I don't think she is behind what happened to Nadia." Zayan's fists curled immediately.

"Sweet?" He asked, unamused, sitting up straight.

"Umm...yeah..." A blush appeared, fuming Zayan's temper.

"You know she is taken, right?" He countered, making the boy's eyes widen in shock. Bahadur gave him a baffled look, but Zayan completely ignored him, keeping his eyes solely on the boy.

"No way," Emir pulled on his chains, pushing his chair slightly away from the round-cafeteria tables.

"She is." Zayan nodded, convincingly. "Some lucky man has already won her heart. Yet, you don't know that. And still, you claim she is innocent...even when this is your sister's case we are talking about." The boy turned speechless for a second.

"Do you think she is behind this?" He then spoke in a small voice, eyed lowered towards the surface of the table.

"Maybe. A naive man really can't trust those eyes." Zayan shrugged, standing up. "Thank you for your help." He smiled. The boy simply accepted the gesture, looking away, eyes almost glossy with emotions.

"Oh, and tight sleeves can't really hide." Saying this, Zayan walked away from the shocked boy with Bahadur hurriedly following behind.

"That was great, sir," He lightly slapped Zayan's back in joy. "That whole 'taken and in love' bluff...the boy seemed like he was hiding something. We, guys, literally missed out on that. He was almost defensive about that girl. We will call him for more questioning."

"Thank you," Zayan smirked. "But, I wasn't really bluffing about the taken part." Winking at his partner, he put his eyeglasses back on and headed back towards his car.

Today had been quite interesting.

Two arms; one clawed by a toddler, one hidden by a tight sleeve...both men knew Nyla. Both had, or knew, people who had hurt Nyla.

How odd?

Sweet Nyla...she truly was interesting.

Late at night, Zayan was studying Nyla's case files...his hat lazily resting on his locks and his feet placed on the side-table. This boosted his mind cells. In the process of investigating this case, he loved how he was getting more insight into his mysterious wife whom he had almost let go of.

What a terrible loss that would have been!

'When little, Nyla used to visit Doctor Sana. Her medical reports show that the girl used to claim to see strange humans with creepy grins and vacant expressions. She was mentally disturbed and would speak to herself, often pulling on her hair to get rid of the thoughts in her head. Doctor Sana had diagnosed her to be suffering from schizophrenia. She claimed that it was a side-effect of her losing a dear friend of hers at a young age.'

Lost a dear friend?

After the death of Doctor Sana, who died from a burglary turned fatal, Nyla was taken to many other doctors.'

How peculiar?

Reading this, Zayan decided it was about to make some calls. He felt like Doctor Sana's death was no coincidence. Despite Nyla being too young at that time to really be accused of anything, he knew that a psychiatrist who had ruled Nyla as a schizophrenic patient must definitely not be on her good side.

What an intriguing twist.

CHAPTER 3

Zayan

"Sir, what are we doing here...being in our casual attires?" Holding on to the handle of Zayan's Mclaren car, Bahadur frowned, eyeing his colleague with confusion.

"Readying my nerves to attend a party," Zayan joked, lazily smiling, leaning against the driving seat of his car and playfully tapping his fingers against the steering wheel. Their car was parked right across the street from a huge house that had been decorated by fairy lights. There were entering this house with fancy party masks covering their faces. A lot of cars had been parked in front of this house and powerful noise and waves of laughter could be heard escaping from it.

Thankfully with all the mayhem, no one was noticing the mysterious black Mclaren, parked under a tree, with tinted windows.

"Ummm, sir, now is not the time to be attending a party..." Bahadur pointed, baffled by what exactly they were doing here.

"Non-sense. Now is a perfect time. Come on." Straightening his collar, Zayan got out of the car and smirked at the feel of what he was going to do. Bahadur quickly jogged beside him.

"Sir-" He had started protesting, but Zayan was just in no mood to listen. Simply waving off the concerns, he headed towards the front entrance of the party house.

As usual, his arrival caught the attention of all the females. Subtle giggles and whispered praises began reaching his ears. Shaking his head while slightly smirking, Zayan stopped to observe the house and area...thinking of ways to make his plan work. There were so many guests showing up at this party, so many different masks...that it was probably difficult for the host to remember them all.

Looking around, while ignoring the Bahadur's consistent questioning of what he was planning to do, he pinched his chin in thought and beamed at the sight of a girl crossing the street to reach the house. She seemed rather shy and awkward, nervous to be entering the party alone. In her hands was a box full of masks.

Bingo...

Quickly heading towards her, with Bahadur rushing behind, he smirked, as he immediately caught the attention of the girl, and watched her stance straightened up; turn more feminine and stylish.

"Yes?" She spoke with hidden eagerness.

Zayan had to hide an amused smile upon having this woman speak even before he had.

"Bella, can I speak to you for a moment?" He asked, playing his charms.

"Sure..." she spoke, sounding so nervous and shy. The street was empty except for a few cars seldom driving by.

"Umm...I don't have a mask, and I see you carrying this box full of masks. Can I borrow two for my friend and me?" He ruffled his locks, giving her his most charming grin while gesturing towards Bahadur who had finally caught up to him. The woman visibly grew awestruck and dazed.

"Yes, of course." She nodded, quickly pulling out two silver eye masks for him. Bahadur scoffed lowly at this display.

Some girls are just too naive.

Eyeing him with amusement, Zayan smiled delightfully at the woman. "Thank you, Bella. Your name?" He asked politely, just to keep her in this heart-eyed stance.

"S-Saira." She responded with a giddy shyness. This woman seemed completely mesmerized. It was quite entertaining to witness. Not bothering to pull her out of her daze, Zayan grabbed the masks with an amused smile and turned towards Bahadur.

"Let's go."

Both of them quickly tied the masks around their head.

Zayan took the lead, as they stepped inside the house.

Inside, the party was raging with guests. The living room had its sofas and cousins pushed back against the wall, and everyone seemed to be having the time of their lives, talking in groups, etc. A young bride and bridegroom were sitting on a sofa placed in the middle of the room.

There were yellow ceiling lights lightening up the room...t he smell of flower bracelets floating in the room. Sweets and chocolates were being passed around along with cans of soft drinks. The hosts were nowhere to be seen, and everyone was too engrossed to wonder about the identity of the powerful men standing near the entrance of the hall. The half-face masks were enough to keep others interest and curiosity at bay.

Now swaying his gaze around the room, Zayan's gaze narrowed on the couple he had been searching for...used the masks for.

'Mr and Mrs Khawar'

His in-laws. Sweet!

He had been feeling a little hesitant to meet them, given how poorly he had treated their daughter, yet upon finally finding them, all the hesitance vanished.

The loveable couple were joining in the celebrations of their niece's wedding. Their daughter was in jail. Yet like the lovely folks they were known to be, they were there to celebrate the joys of others. They weren't wearing masks, eating sweets while standing near the new happy couple, and sharing jokes with the parents of the bride. This behaviour is what he wanted to observe.

He wanted to subtly observe the reaction of sweet Nyla's parents, get to know what kind of people they were and see how they were dealing with the pain of their gentle daughter being in jail. Prison cells are notorious for pain and torture. If the parents truly consider their children weak, tender and harmless, they would be tortured by the fact of having their children subjected to harsh environments. Not that Zayan's heart so fond of real beauty and art would allow any harm to reach that sweet criminal. Her gaze had the power to turn him into a lovestruck fool willing to take a bullet for her heart.

What a powerful woman.

"They are Nyla's parents" Bahadur realized, standing beside him, feeling surprised by the realization. "They look so happy," he observed.

"Yup." Zayan nodded, touching his face mask and then making his way towards a table that was placed at the very backside of the room and filled with treats.

"Coffee..." A pleased smile appeared on his face as he started pouring himself a cup.

"Sir, is that why we are here...to see how her parents are co-oping?" Bahadur spoke, sounding so tangled, eyes still focused on Nyla's parents.

"We have to bring them to the police station for some further questioning. Why not invite them in style?" Zayan mused, taking sweet sips of coffee. Sweet, strong and going straight to his senses; just the way he liked it. His mind felt already stronger by a simple sip.

"I guess..." Bahadur sounded doubtful.

Nobody came near their table because everyone was now busy feeding the bride and groom chocolates and desserts. Zayan watched as Mrs Khawar laughed while feeding the bride some chocolate and teasingly forcing some bangles up her wrist. This woman's daughter was being suspected of m urder..was known to be mentally ill. It was thought-provoking to see her so relaxed.

Was this being used to the pain or something else?

Now having the woman grab a flower bracelet from the basket placed on the table before the couple and her husband handing some money to the groom, Zayan placed back his coffee cup on the table.

"It's time." He gestured to Bahadur who quickly grabbed a doughnut from the table and nodded.

He walked up to the husband, earning whispers from around. Apparently, even masks weren't enough to keep fe-male attention at bay for long.

"Mr Khawar." He called out to the happy father who had just emptied his wallets for the couple.

"Yes?" He turned around, with his happy expressions turning into a frown. "What is the meaning of showing up-"

"I am really sorry for doing this, right now," Zayan quickly spoke. "But I would really like you and aunt to come to the police station tomorrow for some questioning. I thought I should personally come and ask you, guys. I am willing to help Nyla." He offered an earnest look.

Nodding, the father sighed. "Of course."

"She has always been our little, fragile and struggling baby. The first time she was diagnosed completely broke our hearts. When little, she used to get sick so often, and then there were the mental illnesses...your grandfather is a wonderful man, and we never blamed you for not staying with our Naina. It was never your baggage, and we deeply apologise for doing this to you, for being selfish.

We know why you never wanted to do anything with us, but this marriage helped Naina through so much. Our baby is not well. She has been through so much pain, and you have no idea how hard it has been for us, parents, to see that...how long we have struggled to reach this point where we are finally managing to deal with this pain. We will break completely if we don't act normal and distract ourselves." Nyla's mother was crying into the palm of her hand, with her husband sitting next to her.

They were sitting in the interrogation room, with Zayan sitting across from them. Thankfully, all the cameras had been turned off to allow honest confrontation. There was an interrogation table placed in the middle. Plates full of biscuits and a kettle filled to the brim with Coffee had been placed on it to relax his in-laws.

The stressful atmosphere wouldn't be helpful in getting some answers. Zayan wanted them to calm down. It was so strange how he was formally meeting these people just now. At the time of his marriage, he had been too cold and reserve to bother with anyone. He was no longer mad about being trapped into marriage because the sweetest Nyla was worth it. Her gorgeous eyes had bought him.

"Nora, what exactly did you notice that made you feel like Nyla is mentally struggling with issues?" Zayan leaned back against his chair, eyes calculative and alert with knowledge. He was pinching his chin in thought as he waited for her answer.

"My wife and I have already-"

"It's okay. Zayan needs to know." Nora quickly appeased her husband, gently patting his hand.

Sighing, she lowered her gaze towards the table. A small smirk threatened to appear on Zayan's face. He now knew whose traits Nyla had picked.

"She started seeing stuff." She raised her gaze, seemingly lost in a memory. "After the death of her best friend, she started seeing people...randomly talking to them. At first, she called them her friend, making us believe that this was just a way of co-oping for our sensitive baby." Zayan's head tilted at this.

Interesting.

"But then, she started experiencing fits." She sobbed again. "She would scream, cry and tell us about some strange humans who would show up at her room and try to hurt her. We were so worried. We took her to doctors, even considered the possibility of being possessed, but nothing worked until one doctor informed us that our baby was s-schizophrenic." She had a hard time saying those words, moving to quickly hold her husband's hand.

Both she and her husband were looking miserable and in so much pain; their shoulders were slumped in defeat and seemed so burden.

"Soon after that," she still continued, with tears echoing in her tone, "we started getting her treated. We tried everything, even got fooled by some experts and had our sweetest daughter stay in a nearby asylum for a couple of days. Those days were horrible. We don't wish to even think of all the blunders we made out of desperation and extreme pain, pray deeply for our daughter to forgive us." There was so much regret in her tone that Zayan had to make her stop and chew on a piece of biscuit.

Soon, after having her relaxed, he gestured for her to continue with the story. Khawar seemed too upset to reprimand Zayan for making his wife suffer like this.

Good for him.

Sniffing, she heaved a sigh. "Anyhow," there was this strengthening of her soul again, as she composed herself, "Our Nyla started getting better. She talked less about seeing people and started smiling a bit more. In fact, she even began doing jobs, having relaxing long walks in a forest nearby our house and spending time reading her favourite book. We were so happy until our baby got caught up in this mess. Which is so wrong. I am telling you, Zayan, Nyla is innocent! You are already divorcing her. Please don't break her any further! I know how these institutions are...so corrupt and money-brought, so don't damage my daughter to appease your heads and get your revenge," she pleaded, her gaze desperately seeking some understanding, anger hinting to appear.

Her husband was quick to calm her down. "Dear, it's okay. The police will make sure justice is served. Nothing will happen to our Nyla." He cooed, cupping a cup of coffee for her.

Zayan leaned folded, holding his hand and placing them on the table...his gaze was fixated on the vulnerable pair with consideration and a mischievous smile threatening to appear.

"Yes, of course. Nyla will not be wronged. In fact, I kinda find her to be an extremely pleasant woman to be around, now that I have gotten to know her. Do you mind telling me if you are from the northern areas? I heard such beauty exists in those areas." He pointed with a sweet smile, eyebrows narrowed slightly to see if the mother would give him the reaction he wanted.

"Really? Do you like Nyla?" She immediately lost her tears and anger, asking with subtle excitement and enthusiasm, as she sat up straight and ignored her husband's glare.

Perfect.

"Umm...yes, I do." He leaned back, suppressing a loped smile. "But I was wondering..." he feigned a frown, cupping his chin, "You have accepted that you lied to get me married to your daughter, why do you accept mercy from me? Why do you sound so eager at the thought of me liking your fragile daughter? I have clearly mistreated her for a long time. Is a mother's plea to get her daughter settled down after so much pain?" He sharply raised his gaze towards the couple. "Or is it simply the fact that you and my grandpa know more than you let on? I mean if I am so desperately looking for ways to appease my heads and take revenge, then shouldn't you be worried about the safety of your daughter who is currently being kept in this prison cell?" He pointed out. The woman looked speechless for a second.

"N-No..."

"Also," he interrupted while pressed a curled fist against his chin, "I am quite curious about what drove some parents to make blunders such as sending their precious daughter to an asylum. I mean surely her wild imagination wouldn't be enough for two normal and loving parents to grow this desperate. Hmmm?"

"I-yes, you are right." She accepted defeated, lowering her gaze towards the table.

Bullseye.

"Dear-" Her husband began cautioning for her to stop, but she seemed like she needed to make a full confession to make her heart feel at ease.

"Khawar, we have to do this for Nyla." She met her husband's gaze with determination.

"You see, Zayan," she turned to face Zayan again, who was eyeing her with curiosity and suspicion," Nyla has always been a little different. Your grandpa knew about it. He has been Khawar's friend for the longest time." she lowly confessed, lowering her gaze. "When little, she didn't get on well with most children, sobbed about seeing strange humans, was badly affected by her best friend's death. And with all that going on, she had this rather violent fit." Zayan's eyes widened.

"Nothing like that." She was quick to reassure, waving her handly momentarily. "It is just that we once walked into her room and found her standing over an injured cat. She claimed it was those humans, but she was the only one in the room, crying her heart out and had her hands covered in blood. She honestly looked so scared. So as she grew old, for her health and stability, your grandpa suggested marriage

" she explained with a hint of shame. Zayan found himself stiffening with realization.

This was just like those murder scenarios.

The coincidence was uncanny.

"Why did you not tell the police this before?" He asked, accusingly, firmness echoing in his tone, yet he didn't want to sound extremely rude. After all, these were his wife's parents. He didn't have the heart to deal with Nyla's gorgeous eyes being mad at him. Only a few men were brave enough to fight those intense forms of torture.

"Because we know how it would look like." She defended, her voice on the verge of cracking from a bunch of emotions. "We knew that this was something the police would pick as a piece of evidence to frame Nyla. We don't trust the cops, especially when Nyla's late friend was killed in a shooting gone wrong, and I know my baby might have some aggressive fits when little, but even back then, she didn't hurt any human being. It will be unfair to hold her past over her shoulders now." She reasoned.

The mother was making valid points. This did look horribly bad for Nyla.

Zayan chewed on his thumbnails and started pouring himself a cup of coffee. He wasn't really sure.

Was this the case of a psychopath or something more...

Strange humans being sighted...hmmm...

CHAPTER 4

Nyla

I closed my eyes. The screams were loud. The gurgling pain of victims...it wouldn't leave my mind. I was fairly young when they had befriended me. They had appeared out of nowhere, and on when stormy night, when my mother wanted me to be a big girl and sleep without a night light, I had found them sitting in one corner. They were mute, smiling, and I had liked them a lot. For years, I kept them as my secret friends. They wanted me to be my secrets.

Yet, times started to change...as I grew older, their smiles started turning strange. They caught me off guard when they slashed open my cat, horrified me when they lured my best friend into walking towards her murder. That was when I started begging them, hinting my parents about my friends, but they just won't leave me alone.

Every night, they would stay near me and just stare. I had no idea what they were...what they wanted. They wouldn't show up in front of my parents and were selective about the people that got to see them. They had me dreaming nightmare, struggling with severe anxiety and having nervous breakdowns. I thought they would be done with their vicious ways after killing my friend, but I had no idea that they wanted more.

One day, waking up with huge claw marks on my hands had made my heart pound in horror. The dread...the sweat and fear...I had realized that they were targetting me, too. That was the day my trips to the hospital had begun. The first person to know about my condition had deemed me insane. My stay at an asylum had been strangely comforting because, for some reason, they didn't show up there.

With time, I had even picked up their quirks and ways. They showed up only at night time, hated white light, hated having an audience...and they hated me. I would mostly stay out of home at night time, linger near the asylum building to get away from those creatures, but now...I was in another mess because of those creatures. They just wouldn't leave me alone.

I needed help.

Zayan

"Her psychiatrist, Doctor Sana got murdered in a burglary got wrong. She was the one who had long sessions with her. After her death, Nyla rarely opened up. We tried to make her speak, but it felt like she was just dealing with too much to speak." Doctor Haya-head of the Psychological Institute, now folded her hands. She was a woman in her fifties and seemed to be well-aware of Nyla's condition.

"Doctor Haya, what kind of a patient do you deem Nyla to be?" Leaning back on his chair, Zayan chewed on his thumbnail in a thoughtful way. The doctor had just ordered coffee for him. And he was waiting for this cup to really feel energized.

"A shaky one. Many patients suffering from mental issues have these timid and shakiness nerves. She seemed too shaken, too fearful and nervous," the woman spoke. Her voice was a bit high-pitched. Either this woman was lying, or she was getting affected by Zayan's charm.

"Do you believe children can be psychopaths?" He spoke, ignoring her nervousness. Bahadur was waiting for him in the car, and he wanted to be done with this interview. Just one answer. He was just looking for one thing.

"I don't really. I mean there have been child murderers, but they are usually influenced by their family or any other factors. Nyla has wonderful parents." she confessed, seeming hesitant.

Finally, their coffee cups arrived, and Zayan took a moment to take a long sip.

"Hmm..." He placed the silver cup on the table and then leaned back again. He now had a small underlying smile on his face.

"Doctor Sana, your institute has been running for decades and is the most famous in town. Am I correct?"

"Yes," she nodded proudly.

"Then, why is it that you hired a psychiatrist with only one year's training?" He raised one eyebrow arrogantly, causing her stance to immediately start showing nerves.

"Umm...we hire the best. People who show promising talent and brains are hired by us." She explained. This time, a huge grin appeared on Zayan's face.

"Is that so?"

"Yes," The woman awkwardly shifted her scarf.

"So why did Doctor Sana declare Nyla a patient of schizophrenia when clearly she had only a couple of sittings with Nyla? Why was there a rush to label a child so quickly?"

"She was a complicated case. The signs were clear-"

"But she was acting out. You claim children are influenced, but I see none of your medical histories studying Nyla's background. Why not explore her reasons?" He mused.

Doctor Haya looked speechless and caught off guard for a second.

"We did-"

"No. Her medical files mentioned her to be suffering, having fits and experiencing a mental problem, showing signs of schizophrenia, but there are no reasons. Doctor Haya, is it true that you recently fired one doctor because of temper issues?"

"Umm...yes. This shows how professional our atmosphere is."

"A patient complained about that doctor, right?" He added. She nodded.

"But a child may not be able to complain."

"Detective Zayan-"

"Do you have the details of Doctor Sana's medical history?"

"It is confidential."

"But do you?" He now stood up. Doctor Haya looked too caught-off guard to even remember that she had the choice to send him out of the office. Having her turn silent gave him a clear answer. She didn't.

This institute didn't really do background check-ups and had given the doctors, with little experience, complete control over serious cases.

What a shame.

She was waiting for him.

Tipping his hat a little, Zayan hid a smirk and stepped inside the interrogation room. Feeling amused as her mesmerizing eyes tortured his soul by glaring at him. She had no idea how easily she could completely defeat him, ruin him.

"Ah...Nyla...I met your parents, finally," he announced, smiling wide, holding a black coffee mug in his eyes. He moved to sit down on the chair placed before her table and took a sip, watching her grow surprised.

"You called in mom and dad?"

"Yes. I had to ask them some questions. But don't worry, I was a complete gentleman in front of them, even smiled when your mom wanted us to make amends." He joked, gaze searching for her reaction. He had hinted that he no longer wished to divorce her.

Her eyes widened. "What the heck! You are lying. My mom would never..." She sounded so embarrassed and shocked.

"Am I?" He raised one eyebrow, shaking her confidence.

She scowled in irritation. "Mr Zayan, I am exhausted-"

"Zayan..." He corrected her, but she didn't even bother with it.

"Kindly, tell me how far you have reached with this case. If you want to involve my family in this, then I am out. The only reason I am here is that I want this to be kept away from my family...to find the truth for those who have suffered. My parents have dealt with a lot because of me. You are pretty aware of that. I don't want you to involve them in this."

"Well, you are right." He accepted, leaning back in his chair. "I also visited that old Psychology institute that you used to visit. Do you remember Doctor Sana?" He took another sip of coffee.

"Yes." The hostility in her stance was what Zayan wanted to see.

Interested, he placed the coffee mug down and then abruptly leaned forward, folding his arms on the table.

"Nyla, was Doctor Sana of any good?" He spoke, grinning wide.

She seemed quite weirded out by his expressions now. Pushing her chair slightly away, she hesitantly nodded. "Yes, she was a good doctor."

"No," he shook his head, loving the effect her fragile stance was having on him. She seemed like a trapped lamb. Cute. "I am talking about if she was a good person."

"We must not talk ill about the deceased." She immediately countered. He hid a smirk and leaned back.

"Touche..." He accepted. Nyla hadn't realized, but she had just confessed that Doctor Sana was not a good person.

"How did you feel when she claimed that you were schizo-phrenic?" He then mused, eyeing her expressions.

"I was disappointed." She began fidgeting.

"But did you feel raging mad?" He countered, folding his hands and sitting up straight.

"Mr Zayan, what are you trying to say-"

"Were you murderously mad?" He continued. The immediate show of her temper almost had his heart squeezed with fondness.

This woman...

"Mr Zayan...if you think I murdered that woman, you are insane." She stood up, glaring hotly at him. "That woman got murdered in some arm burglary attack. I was too young at that time...too tiny. Have some shame before passing such comments-"

"But she had the same marks as the victims who got murdered in the forest," he countered, standing up too, hiding an amused look.

"Yes, but not every mark means something! You are a detective, so use your brains!" She scolded. She was so tiny yet so full of anger.

"Bella, that woman declared you unstable. Are you sure that you were fine with that judgement? That it didn't bother you one bit?" He pointed, knowingly

"She was just doing her job!" She hit her fists against the table.

"And are you okay with the way she was doing her job?"

"Yes, of course, I was." She threw her hands up in the air.

"Are you sure?"

"Yes!" she bellowed.

"Do you love me?" he threw in, smiling as he saw her get completely caught off guard.

"What? No!" She quickly shook her head, looking so adorably mad.

"Ouch." Chuckling slightly, he sat down and started drinking coffee again. A mischievous smile was playing on his face, as he watched from under his eyelashes, saw her working to compose herself and then sitting down.

Her temper was still fuming, her eyes so intense and captivating.

"Mr Zayan..." She was not done with him yet. "I did not murder that woman. She was doing her job. I knew that this was all part of her training, but you are right. I did hate her," she confessed, placing curled fists on the table. "I hated her ragingly, intensively and sadistically."

CHAPTER 5

Z ayan

Sitting on his office chair, with the cop radio playing in the background, Zayan leaned back and held Nyla's casefile before his face. He was chewing on a piece of mint candy, with his cup of steaming hot coffee placed on the desk before him. Only the table lamp, placed on one corner of his desk, was lit, and with the yellow-lamp light casting shade on his face, he was comfortably lost in his train of thoughts.

Nyla, her gaze...the mystery held in them had him continuously getting distracted. His wife's case had been such a plot twist in his life. Apparently, people with power, who had indirectly harmed Nyla, were sporting the same scars as the victims of the Embalian Killings, yet it was declared that their scars had nothing to do with Nyla. Emir, that college boy, he didn't hold a grudge against his sister's supposed murderer, and Nyla...a beautiful and sweet doe...she claimed to be capable of holding hate.

Zayan read the name of the asylum-she had once been kept in-and smirked.

'Central Mental Asylum for Embalians'

It was the same asylum he had stayed during his case trials-after five years of staying in prison in order to preserve a woman's lie. His lawyer had been nervous and an inexperienced guy who had the court consider Zayan's crime to be a consequence of mental health issues. After weeks of frustration spent in the asylum, Zayan had finally decided to defend his own case.

His first court hearing, with him as a lawyer, immediately convinced the judge of his innocence. In fact, the judge's niece, who had been part of the jury, later sent him a bouquet, expressing her interest in becoming his wife. He had smirked at such a proposal. He had continued receiving those bouquets for a long time; that woman had been thoroughly impressed.

Anyhow, his days at the asylum were actually coincidental with the time Nyla's stayed at the asylum. He wondered how he had never noticed such a devastatingly and captivating mystery being in such close proximity, but then again, if he had known about her existence, he would have probably decided to just stay in the asylum.

Chuckling while shaking his head at such a thought, he kept reading the case file until Bahadur (who had been sitting on a couch placed on a few feet before his desk; pushed against the left-side wall, with its right side facing the desk.) loudly shifted the open newspaper pages gripped tightly in his hands and spoke, "some Embalians disgust me. There is news about two Embalian men who killed some natives in Chandelia. They got caught by the Chandelain armed force at the airport. Turns out, these Embalians were working for our rebel team. Such shame for our country." He scoffed indignantly while reading the front page news.

Zayan placed the Nyla's case file on the desk and pinched his chin in a thoughtful way, eyeing Bahadur from underneath his eyelashes.

"Bahadur, you are an extremely patriotic man, right?" He mused, leaning further against the back of his chair as he silently observed Bahadur's reaction.

"Yes, sir..." Immediately, Bahadur's stance echoed pride and honour, as he placed the newspaper on the couch's arm and turned to face Zayan. " My great grandfather lost his life in the great Embalian's war fought against the Chandelians. My family has spent decades serving our country. I am working hard to do the same." He announced, momentarily shaking his fist while raising his chin to prove a point. This was a man from a pure army background

"Then, why is it you are too quick to believe in the news that believes our nation was shamed?"

"I-I-"

"The Chandelians have framed our people so many times, so why are you too quick to believe words instead of searching for the truth?" Zayan continued pointing out; his expressions innocent, nonchalant, as he took a quick sip of coffee and then folded his hands behind his head, gazing up at the ceiling as he listened to Bahadur's explanation.

"Sir, this news has been gathered from an authentic response-"

"But why do we do it?" Zayan spoke, still looking at the ceiling, being so lost in thought. "There was news in the paper today about children being murdered by 'supposed' rebels...rebels being killed by officers....men dying to protect others; why believe in this news and simply shrug it off with self-determined judgement, instead of working to find the truth about how human lives really got lost? Why do we favour other's words over our own?"

"Umm..." Bahadur seemed speechless now.

Zayan suppressed an amused smirk at this reaction. Many really didn't get how his mind worked. He used to score perfect grades in his exams, but when it came to being a student in the class...most of his teacher considered him a bored and-lost in his own world-kind of a student whose questions they always failed to answer. He had stopped asking when he had picked on the fact that his teachers struggled to meet with his mental capacity.

"Is it because it is easy to hate than understand and listen?" He then straightened up again, looking at Bahadur while taking another quick sip of coffee.

"Maybe, sir," Bahadur spoke, awkwardly.

"Do you know sweet Nyla used to hate her psychiatrist..." He continued, a suppressed smile teasing his expressions.

"Oh, about that case, how far are you, sir, from cracking it?" Bahadur asked instead, growing alert and attentive. His shaky stance immediately got replaced by his work mode.

"I am 10 percent closer," Zayan shrugged, grabbing the case file and lazily skimming through its pages.

"Oh, okay. Mind if I grab something from your kitchen?" Bahadur stood up.

"Sure."

He was on the last sip of his coffee, continuously tapping his chin with his pen when Bahadur stepped back inside the office, carrying a huge white box in his hands.

"Sir, I was just looking around when I found this in your cupboard-"

"You were snooping around?" Zayan spoke, raising one eyebrow while folding his hands and placing his elbows on the desk.

"I-I-"

"Some females tend to get carried away by their delicate emotions and decide to give me gifts. I don't really know them, but I like keeping those gifts..." Zayan spoke, mischievously. The box was just one of the few boxes full of gifts that had been sent to him. He had been receiving expensive gifts, wristwatches, chocolates, perfumes, cards, bouquets, ever so often by females who didn't really know him but had, somehow, got infatuated by him. He had so many secret fans.

"But, there is a court case file in it..." Bahadur frowned. This time, Zayan couldn't help but chuckle, as smugness and haughty confidence echoed in his smile.

"I got a random sue notice from some man whose two daughters had her heartbroken because they heard a rumour about me getting married. It was strangely sweet, so I decided to keep a copy. I am a sentimental guy." He shrugged unapologetically.

Bahadur stared agape. "But, sir, this is wrong. You can't accept these gifts."

"They come with no return address."

"I-I-"

"Bahadur, I have decided what we are going to do next. This case file doesn't really mention any notes of officers visiting the crime place with Nyla. Can you give me details about that?" Zayan then changed the topic, chewing on his thumbnails, as he lowered his gaze towards the desk to fully focus on Bahadur's words.

"Umm...sure," Bahadur seemed caught-off-guard by this abrupt change of topic. "We did send some officers, alone in the forest to see what really happens in the time-frame that the murders take place, but usually nothing shows up. No animal attacks take place. Nothing. One of our officers did claim to have almost got bitten by a snake, but usually, the animals stay in the hiding. And no one really took Miss Nyla along because she really didn't trust us from purposely framing her. We really don't know how to make her crack."

Zayan tilted his head in thought, momentarily closing his eyes. "So she doesn't want to visit the forest with the police task..."

"Yes, sir." Bahadur nodded. "We asked her if she would accompany our team to the forest. We had cameras and everything."

Hearing this, Zayan looked up sharply at the Bahadur. "What if only two officers go along with her? No cameras and weapons to be taken along..."

"But, sir, that is highly dangerous. Also, I don't think that our suspect will co-operate with us on that."

"Of course, but it might just solve our case." Zayan pointed, leaning back in his chair, with the coffee flowing in his veins, his brain was coiling with hints, analysis and ideas. If he had to know how exactly the murders worked, he had to enact scenarios that led to people getting killed.

So the murders occurred at night, with no audience, no camera presence and Nyla as the sole witness. Zayan would have to see if those murders still occurred when there were two witnesses present. Nyla didn't trust the police. She didn't enjoy the idea of a team and camera sets accompanying her to the forest. But she would most definitely not mind him and another officer accompanying her to the forest. She claimed she wanted to find the truth. Let's see how eager and willing she was to search for the truth.

Zayan smiled in amusement as he thought about how he was going for a long walk in the forest. Maybe, Nyla would torture his emotions further by arrogantly not bothering with his attempt to find the truth. He would be a complete goner if she haughtily raised her chin and announced him to be not worthy of witnessing her favourite place. That woman knew how to crush hearts.

He kept reading her case study, wondering what exactly her reaction was going to be at this offer.

Nyla

I woke up with a heavy heart. Dried tears were flowing down my cheeks, as memories of my past echoed in my mind in the form of dreams. I had just dreamt about how my best friend's murder again. That sight wouldn't leave my mind. It had been haunting me for years, and the look in her eyes when she had collapsed...it had been torturing me.

I had been struggling, hurting for a long time, and often, this terror used to make me so lonely because no one around me really understood. I had been fighting this pain for such a long time, and being in a constant state of being terrified and mentally abused by the strange creatures had me exhausted.

There were often tears shed, and I had to wipe them away. My friends, my loved ones...I couldn't really be with anyone because of the creatures tormenting my days. And sadly, no one bothered with my pain anymore. It was easy for everyone to distract themselves from my pain because my suffering was just too painful to be dealt with. But, just because everyone turned their backs at me, doesn't mean I didn't need them. I needed everyone, my old life, love, emotions, but I couldn't afford those luxuries. I had my own battle to fight...all alone.

Even the man, whom I called my husband, had been just another heartache for me. I thought my chapter with him was over until the police decided to involve the infamous Detective Zayan in solving my case. It had been so embarrassing being questioned and interrogated like a criminal by my husband

The moment I had found out that he was the one going to investigate my case, I had been crushed. More humiliation and self-degradation. The man choosing to divorce me had been given the perfect reason for doing so.

Super!

However, being a fighter, I had decided to seal all emotions and pretend like I didn't know him at all, as I allowed him to handle my case. I was good at that. It had destroyed me when he had claimed he wanted to divorce me, yet I never blamed him because I knew my demons were too strong. No one deserved carrying my baggage.

He never gave me a chance, and I never asked for it.

Though, now that he was getting more deeply involved with my case, he had been acting so irritatingly strange. He was being so nonchalant about how we really never got along, how he had chosen to simply leave. His sudden praising of my eyes, blatant weird questions, they were so confusing. I couldn't understand what he really wanted. He was up to something, and I couldn't understand what.

He was setting a trap for me, and it hurt that my scars hadn't even allowed me to be truly adored by someone. I was a supposed criminal being trapped by my own husband. How embarrassing, pitiful and just so lonesome...

Sitting up straight, I moved to grab a glass of water and tried to relax my thoughts. The air was windy and cool. I knew that as a wise soul I should be enjoying the breeze, but I was just feeling incredibly low today.

It was about time to visit the forest with that extremely bold detective and another female officer. I had only decided to accept their demand for visiting the forest with me because I didn't want to have that annoyingly smug Zayan question my sincerity in having this case solved and gloat about why he had made the right choice by leaving me. I was truly heartbroken for the lives that had been lost in the process.

Also, only that detective and a lady officer were really going to accompany me with no cameras, recording sets or weapons (which usually triggered the creatures), so if anything did happen, there would be no such proof of me being involved in any murderous plans. It would all be just a coincidence, yet again. I would play it like that. No one would really believe my truth. I had tried telling it before...so many times.

I was still quite worried about visiting the forest again, with no white light or anything. Zayan might be considered smart, but he was making an extremely foolish mistake by purposely choosing an obvious way of getting mauled. The creatures would appear. I was sure of it. And these foolish people...they weren't going to be spared. Instant concern and worry for Zayan panged my heart, but I quickly squashed it.

I wasn't supposed to worry about him. He was so smug, blatant and overconfident, ridiculing my emotions ever so often, having the audacity to ask me if I loved him while actually interrogating me...ugh, he screamed arrogance. I was in so much pain, and all he could think of making me boast his ego. It was disrespectful. In fact, his actions annoyed me more because I was aware that his charming approach was just the way he was with all women. Yet, despite the irritation, I knew that even he didn't deserve to become a victim of some creepy creatures.

No one deserved to become a victim of my battle.

Tangled with the tension and stress of how to save people without making many consider me insane, I jolted slightly as a police officer rattled my prison door and announced that it was time to head to the forest.

There was no way I could prevent this walk from happening now.

CHAPTER 6

Nyla

With a young female office, Officer Rida, walking by my side and Zayan walking ahead, I was slowly heading towards the depth of the Embalian forest while trying to keep my calm. It was dark, terrifying, with a simple torchlight lighting the way. Both Rida and Zayan were carrying baseball bats, while I had my hands tied behind my back- just in case.

It was terrifying.

The night moon was howling across the deep depths of the forest, and the animals seemed to be echoing whispers of terror. Each creak and crispy crushing of the leaves haunted my soul. I knew what was going to happen. Zayan was confident, calm and in an extremely happy mood, but I knew what we were heading towards. The gulps that constantly arose with that feeling had me breathless.

I kept staring at the ground, as I walked, feeling my heart constantly jump up in my throat as the fear had me trembling.

Not again. The thought of witnessing yet another murder, hearing the sound of the shrieks of people whom I knew getting mauled and bleeding towards their dead before my eyes, had my soul pushing me to retreat. But I couldn't.

The terror and the trauma of thinking about how I could feel if that creature hurt Rida...Zayan made me feel faint. Even if he had never cared, I didn't want him to get hurt.

My usual was something that would traumatize me on a daily basis.

I tried keeping my breath calm to keep me from hyperventilating, kept silent to control my emotions. The wind was blowing softly. There were thick bushes and old trees around us, yet the forest canopy was easy enough to observed. We weren't going to become animal preys here.

"Ladies, it is a fine time for a long walk, isn't it?" Zayan suddenly joked without looking back at us, causing Rida to giggle in a feminine manner. I stayed quiet, simply staring at the floor, my heart depressed and helpless.

"I don't mind long walks," Rida spoke with a sweet smile escaping into her tone.

"What about our sweetest criminal? Nyla, are you enjoying going on this long walk with me?" He momentarily looked back, an amused smile being suppressed on his face. I simply rolled my eyes, turning my face away from him.

Annoying!

However, somehow, Zayan's comment didn't settle well with Rida, and I could feel her glaring at me.

"Detective Zayan, Nyla shouldn't really be enjoying anything. I just hope she cooperates with us tonight. I wouldn't stop myself from raising a fist if she dares to step out of the line," she hotly threatened. I clenched my jaw, still not choosing to respond.

The situation didn't demand it.

My heart and soul was worried about so many other things.

This woman was just being an ignorant fool.

Soon, the rest of the walk turned into officer Rida trying to impress Detective Zayan while belittling me. She would snarkily demean me for being a criminal, share heroic episodes of her young days, and Zayan would politely listen to her compete for his attention with an amused stance. There was no point in defending myself. Having so many people think horrible about me, was a norm. I had learned a long time ago that my worries were much more than feeling petty emotions.

There was momentary thought of how this woman was being sweet with my husband, and in a normal situation, a wife would have raged with jealousy. But when one has been fighting alone for so long, they can't really afford to be jealous-especially over a man who had already rejected them.

We were the main meadow when Rida started about her visit to about one of her memorable trips. This woman was rich. Her adventures and tales of having explored so many countries of the world had my heart wonder about how I was missing out on so many experiences because of some deadly creatures. The world sounded so beautiful, but I didn't have the time to explore it.

"The fairy meadow near lake Saiful Malook is so beautiful. You have to visit it."

"Definitely. I will visit it, but you have to assure me that it is as beautiful as our Nyla's eyes." Zayan spoke mischievously, momentarily turning his head back. I could hear him hiding a laugh. He was clearly having fun with this, purposely teasing Rida, enjoying how she was clearly getting agitated by him sparing me his attention.

His remark made me fume.

What was he playing at?

"Detective Zayan, I think it is better if we focus on this situation-"

"I can assure you that it is extremely beautiful," Rida interrupted, completely ignoring his remark about my eyes. I curled my fists in annoyance. These people were really testing my temper. This woman was acting immature. I had to stop myself from becoming part of this ridiculous game.

Irritated, my expression suddenly tightened into a vulnerability, as I realized where exactly we were. Seeing the entrance of the meadow had me snapping back to focus on the dire severe nature of the situation.

We were almost near the place where it all would begin...

My heart raced as I heard my breath growing erratic. These fools had no idea what they were heading towards. The trees around me had started rocking with an eerie sensation. I could feel the tension...the terror.

Blanching slightly, I forced myself to keep on moving as I ignored the carefree moods of the people walking alongside me. Since my hands were tied and no howls of wild animals echoed from near us, Zayan and Rida seemed relaxed. They weren't picking on how silent the air was.

Shoot!

Soon, Zayan pushed up one thick bush and held it up for Rida and me to pass. I was feeling too pale, too faint to do anything. With just a few more steps, we all were standing right in the middle of the meadow-the same meadow where the creatures were about to start with their killings.

Zayan turned to face us and spoke in a joking manner. "Well, ladies, this is it."

I gulped sharply.

Zayan...

The air was still. The clock was ticking, and Zayan just stood a few steps beside me, on my right side, calmly observing his surroundings while Rida, standing on my left side, had grabbed my arm in a firm manner.

Everyone was just waiting with the torchlight switched off. Zayan and Rida were waiting for any signs of danger, any hint of what happened on this meadow, and I was feeling faint with the dread of experiencing the moment when the creatures would appear. If they didn't, it would just solidify Zayan's suspicion that I was behind the murders, but if they did, and Zayan and Rida ended up dying with me again being considered a suspect; though, there would be no proof to confirm my crimes-yet again.

My mind felt so numb, terrified

The situation was so tricky. But, instead of being able to focus on my intense anxiety, I was watching the trees that were a few feet before us lining the borders of this meadow, was feeling wildly aware of my surrounding. It was hard to breathe, do anything because seeing those creatures always terrified my heart...my soul.

It was a torturous experience going through this same pain over and over again. Those haunting screams...the looks of blank tortured eyes staring back at me...they almost had me cupping my ears and curling into a small ball. But there were people watching. I wonder how the creature would react upon finding two hunts of the day.

Zayan and Rida did have small talks with each other to pass the time. My expressions, my mannerism was constantly being scrutinized. I know I was being observed and my behaviour was being secretly analyzed, but I could focus on nothing else except the trees before me; my mood pale and looks dishevelled by the feeling of fear.

I knew that we wouldn't leave this place until the clock struck a minute after the time that the murders had taken place here. Thus, with numb nerves, dread in my heart and terror roaring in my eyes, I kept mutely staring at the trees with a blank expression, desperately stopping myself from hyperventilating until I heard a scratching sound echoing in the air.

My eyes widened; my heartbeat pained.

They were here.

"Zayan," In a moment of desperation, I grabbed onto his hand and sharply looked at him. This had been so wrong. I didn't want anyone to get hurt.

"Nyla...what's wrong?" He looked down at me with a concerned look.

Zayan and Rida didn't notice the sound of nails being scratched against the thick wooden trunks of the trees, couldn't hear them because these creatures could only be heard and seen by me. I could hear tree branches being roughly shuffled...aching by the weight of claws abusing them.

"It is just too dark." I eeped, letting go of his hand. It was too late.

He gave me a thoughtful look, sharply swaying his gaze around our surrounding.

"We will go back soon."

Weakly nodding, I turned around to look at the forest lining again.

There was dim moonlight casting light on this meadow, but the trees were engulfed by the darkness. My breath started turning frantic as I witnessed shadows now climbing down the trees; dark, cunning and malicious.

Zayan and Rida had gone back to discussing some work business, not picking on what was really happening. I couldn't alert them now, say anything because this would just aggravate the creatures.

Frozen while holding in my breath, I mutely watched as the shadows slowly started crawling towards us. They were sporting those blank wide grins, had their eyes shadowed by maniac emotions and were digging their claws into the ground.

Seeing them near almost had me tug on Zayan sleeve in fear and terror. We had to go. Now! They were going to attack. However, just as I was about to start hyperventilating and scream for caution, with a shock, I noticed something strange happening.

The creatures had stopped mid-way. All of them were now looking at Zayan who was laughing while talking to Rida over my head. I immediately snapped my head to look at Zayan, wanting to know what he was doing that had the creatures halted. However, as I turned towards him, my eyes widened as I realized that Zayan was doing absolutely nothing. He seemed quite unaware of what was going around him; even looking at me with a soft look on his face.

He noticed my tense expressions and frowned. "Nyla, what is going on?"

Mutely shaking my head, I ignored Zayan curious expressions and turned to look at the creatures again, only to feel astonished at the sight of them now back-tracking away from us. Their gazes were focused solely on Zayan, and they were surprisingly supporting a deep frown on their face. Their expressions were different. It almost seemed as if they were scared, with their hands now curled and dug in the ground.

What the heck!

I kept watching with sheer astonishment and disbelief as the creatures hurriedly moved back to the forest trees, not even daring to turn their back towards Zayan. They were terrified. Even crushing each other's feet on the way as they made it to the forest line and hurriedly started disappearing in the shadows again.

It was such an astonishing sight to see.

However, just as the last one rushed to hide, it momentarily looked back at me just before disappearing and gritted its sharp teeth in menace. This time, I could see the scorching fury and deep anger in its eyes. It was furious at me for bringing Zayan here.

What the heck was happening!

CHAPTER 7

N yla

A steaming hot cup of coffee was placed before me. There was silence in the air. I felt quiet. After the episode in the forest, Zayan and Officer Rida had escorted me back to the police station and had wait in the interrogation room. I was to be interrogated again.

The absence of something happening made me eligible for being questioned again. Now that nothing happened...I had to explain myself.

There was a shock of what had happened in the forest. The fearful look on those creatures faces when they had seen Zayan...it had me so confused and baffled. What was about Zayan's overconfident and frank personality that had terrified such malicious beings?

I was relieved when nothing happened to him or Rida.

Fidgeting with my fingers while being lost in thought, I looked up as the interrogation door opened. Zayan stepped in while humming a little whistle. He seemed in a good mood, holding a coffee mug in one hand as his gaze reached me. I looked away, instantly.

Since he shared some sort of connection with the creatures, I didn't feel like calling him with formal labels out loud. Zayan was enough now. My emotions had been triggered,

"I knew I could convince you to have coffee with me," he smirked, eyeing the coffee cup placed before me. I rolled my eyes to the right for a second; my frown deepened.

This man...

He had rejected me without even seeing me and was now teasing me so carefreely at all chances...

He was so infuriating!

Ruffling his hair while chuckling lightly at my expressions, he smiled a jolly grin and sat down on the chair placed before my desk, propping one elbow on the desk and cupping his face with one hand. His expressions held a gleam of childish mischievousness, as he placed his coffee mug on the table.

He was up to something.

"So did you enjoy our long walk?" He spoke with a hint of humour.

I simply lowered my eyes and curled my fists before me. I was not going to let this man get to me. I was not going to allow him to use my temper as a weapon. I had to remain calm.

"You know..." He then leaned back against the chair, sensing my silence and grabbing his coffee cup from the table. "I was wondering about what exactly happened in the forest." He nonchalantly took a sip from the mug, yet his attention was sharply on me with a knowing gleam. "Did something happen before the clock ticked for us to go back?"

"As you saw, nothing happened today," I spoke through a clenched jaw. I knew he had caught on to something. He was testing me, seeing how much I was willing to share.

"I don't know, but I didn't like it when these beautiful eyes held so much fear for a second." He placed the coffee mug back on the mug and placed both of his hands on the table with an abrupt motion, folding them with interest and sharp knowledge. This time, he openly showed attention, a low smirk echoing in his tone.

Why on earth were the creatures afraid of this annoying man!

"I-"

"From what I saw...something did happen. But don't worry, I have a feeling that you are not a criminal. In fact, your parents made a huge mistake by sending you to the asylum."

The mention of the asylum immediately caused all anger and annoyance to immediately vaporize, as a strong feeling of misery, shame and hurt engulfed me. Some memories...their reminder was excruciating. I didn't like people talking about it. They were reminders of why I never blamed Zayan for never going me a chance.

I lowered my head slightly as I eyed my hands with a rather defeated expression. The day I was sent to the asylum was still clear. My parents had dropped me off. My mother had been crying, my father...he was putting on a brave facade for the family.

The memories of the first day of staying in an asylum were still so fresh. I remember standing in the shades with the asylum warden standing beside me and holding my shoulder, watching my parents drive away. They had promised me that I would get better in that place.

It had been a cloudy day. I had felt so quiet and alone. There was a single tear rolling down my cheeks, as I had silently wondered how my mother had failed to believe my truth. There was nothing wrong with me. I felt like my own family had sent me away, discarded me for normalcy.

My cousins, my aunts, parents...everyone would get to meet and be together, while I would spend days in such a cold place and feel so utterly alone.

The first few days spent in that place had been so devastatingly terrifying. I would find my hair getting pulled on in the cafeteria, with no one to stop the offenders. My room was so small, and at exactly 12 am, the tube lights would be switched on and the place would turn eerie silent, with distant laughs or cries echoing in the air. Such moments would make me shiver. Those were the moments I would wonder why...why my family never got to know how scared I was...why they were willing to send me so far away from them. W-why were they not able to chase away the monsters for me?

Why did they allow me to fight alone...not believe my fears?

I cared about my family. I thought they knew, so why were they never able to see my fears, able to pull me out of this misery and lead me away from the shades?

I was so lost and terrified. Like a little child, I would beg to be comforted by my family's hug. Yet, for them, I was pretending to be strong and willing. How could no one ever pick on how genuinely scared and weak I was? How desperately I wanted my family to embrace my pain and wipe away my tears.

There were insecurities about me judging if my pain had been too much of a burden for my family if staying in a completely foreign place where people had lost their sanity was what fitted my crowd. We would be allowed to go out for walks in the evening, and I would simply sit on a swing and wonder about the chills.

However, strangely, with the misery becoming a norm, I had noticed that the creatures...they had stopped showing up at night. This was a cue that made me think that perhaps my parents had been right, yet even then I couldn't share my giddy moments of epiphany with them.

Soon, with the realization that the creatures wouldn't bother me in this place, I had started cherishing the feeling of being safe at night. I started calling my parents, adoring normalcy with so much joy. Unfortunately, this was just momentarily. Once I returned back home, the creatures were back.

"I have stayed in that asylum, too." Zayan now snapped me out of my thoughts, making me slightly raise my head in surprise. "In fact, it was during that time you were staying in that place. And might I add, not meeting you there, it was a chance missed by me." He joked. This information shocked me.

What?

Zayan had to stay in that asylum, too. He was there when I was being treated in that place. An epiphany hit me hard. A connection was made in my head. Was that the reason why the creatures didn't show up at that place? Was it because they knew Zayan was staying there? But, the creatures did show up in the police station. Maybe, they were unaware of Zayan being present here. Still, it was all so confusing.

Why Zayan?

My husband...the man I had married out of pure circumstances and didn't much of...why did that man suddenly become so inclined with my experiences?

I still couldn't understand what was about him that had the creatures so fearful and anxious.

"Why were you staying the asylum?" I couldn't help but ask out of curiosity. I wanted answers, something to solve this mystery. My husband had turned out to such a surprise. I had searched my life for reasons, and here this stranger was proving me so many tidbits.

His grandfather had never mentioned anything of this sort. He had got Zayan married to me because he was my father's best friend. I had always thought that his grandfather was being so generous to get his rich, powerful and well-settled grandson to married to me since my parents were worried that I might never get settled because of my issues. Now it seemed like there was something more going on here.

"Let's just say you women know how to become a man's greatest weakness. To be honest, there was nothing I could do to defend myself from such a defeating charm. Even now, just a simple smile-" Zayan mused. The smirk was prominent again. "-can be my ruination. I am a man that really can't refuse a lady's sweet request to be spared pardon."

He was talking about me. He was mocking me by how he could offer me a chance to be pardoned if I pleaded. Ugh! He was playing a game.

"Zayan-"

"I know you haven't committed these murders, Nyla," he spoke before I could scold him, catching me off guard.

He did?

However, just as he had made this announcement, the interrogation door opened again and this time another officer stepped in a hurry.

"Sir, one of the forensic reports of the victims most recently killed in the Embalian Forests. One of these reports includes the reports of a victim whose head was also bashed along with having claw scars on his hands."

"What about these reports, Bahadur?" Zayan quickly stood up after taking one quick gulp of coffee from his mug and turned to face the officer.

"Sir, traces of paint were found in the wounds on the victim's head, and not just any paint...the paint matched the colour-coating of Miss Nyla's baseball bat."

Immediately, Zayan head snapped back towards me again.

"I am madly in love with you."

What the heck!

"What?" My eyes were widened with surprise and disbelief.

After hearing such shocking, terrible and mindblowing news, these were the first words that came into Zayan's mind. Even Bahadur seemed so utterly confused and shocked upon hearing these words. What was Zayan thinking? The shock and disbelief were so immense.

Was he really joking at a time like this?

Unlike other times, his stance showed that he was completely serious and sincere, which meant I had to gulp and muster the possibility of his absurd declaration being true.

Chapter 8

Nyla

The stunned silence was prominent in the air. Both Bahadur and I were sporting an agape look. Shocked and slightly disturbed, especially when Zayan was offering none of his usually mischievous and knowing smirks.

The clicking of the tick from some corner of this room was prominent in the air.

"Look, I hold some suspicion that you have not committed these crimes, but you are hiding something." He then started making his case. "The police have just collected some evidence that proves you guilty. Now there will be no will of yours involved to keep you here. The court will charge you. I can help you. Let's not get divorced. I will defend your case. I will prove that you are innocent. I have done that before. I am good with words...with convincing. Just love me in return, and I won't let anything happen to you." A small confident smile appeared on his face. He looked amused at seeing me trapped.

"I-I don't understand. Is he even allowed to say this?" I turned towards Bahadur.

However, before that man could respond, Zayan stepped in the view again and leaned forward on my table.

"Nyla, I am in charge of this case. I don't like many listening ears..." he spoke, a hint of a smirk echoing in his tone, showing how truly no other policeman had barged into this room. That meant no one of the policemen, except Bahadur, could hear our conversation.

"Umm...."

"I will defend you in court. We can work as a team."

"Zayan, is this all a joke to you?" Anger and hurt caught me.

"Nyla-"

"Your attitude, how casual you about making such decisions, do you have an idea how painful and degrading this all is for me?! You left. Soon after our marriage, I learned that my husband had just left. Do you have any idea how embarrassing, and now you want to jolt in like all is alright like you didn't wreck my emotions and humiliated me in the worst ways possible? I might not care enough about our bond, but I am not a game..."

"I know." His sombre voice caught my attention. "I know, Nyla. I was wrong to leave you." His eyes earnestly met mine. "Just because I didn't know you, was angry at my family, gave me no right to abandon you. I was a heartless prick, but now If you offer me a second chance, I will take care of this case. It will be easier to look to search for hints, clues together...and besides, I am never letting you go." He shrugged in a nonchalant and obvious way, backing away from the table. I scowled slightly, though his words had triggered my emotions.

He was simply being annoying again, yet there was something about his smugness, vulnerability and confidence that then made me tilt my head and think.

He was apologizing...

Somehow, this man had managed to scare away those vicious creatures. There was something about him that made them shake and tremble. If I did give our marriage a chance, then I could manage to keep those creatures at bay. There could be a chance. And he was right about me needing serious help, now that some evidence had been found against me, so I had to make the next moves with caution.

Yet the thought of loving Zayan, such an overly frank, smug and confident man who was well-aware about his charm seemed overwhelming. He had been reckless with me, and I had a lot of things going on to start worrying about tender emotions.

My mental health was deteriorating. Each day, I would wonder about my family and imagine living with them. With age, I held no grudges against my family. This was my battle, yet I did feel lonely and missed being normal. I-I didn't even think any man would want to stick with me, given I was so publically called out for having mental issues, but this man now did. In fact, he was persistent about it.

My relatives used to get mocked how no good-family boys would choose me. While my cousins had people demanding their hand-in-marriage, my parents would be taking me to the doctors. My insanity was popular in the family. It was Zayan's grandfather who momentarily took care of my self-respect.

"Okay," I spoke after a minute of silence, lowering my gaze to my fidgeting hands, my stance almost defeated, still not over the hurt. "I accept."

"What?"

"I forgive you."

Ignoring Bahadur's shock, Zayan simply chuckled in a low tone and softly muttered. "Good."

Mugs of coffee were brought in.

Zayan decided to have a small celebratory party to cele-brate our reunion, He prevented my arrest by cleverly encoun-tering the accusations and evidence with the claim that the matching paints had not been strong enough evidence, and that the claw marks were the real reasons behind the victims' deaths, so freedom was still a right to be enjoyed by me.

Secretly, I then was escorted to some farmlands owned by Zayan with the help of Bahadur. Some of the police officers had been taken into confidence about this planning. I had to be taken back to the police station after the party.

Since I didn't want my family to get involved in this, I was allowed to stay in one of the police quarters. I could leave that quarter at any time-till the verdict was given. Yet, now I couldn't leave the town.

To defend my case, Zayan had to relinquish his authority over it. There would be a chance of bias-ness if he kept acting as the police's detective and my lawyer. For now, he was going to work as solely my lawyer; be my supportive husband.

He was a reputable man with charm and power, so it was easy for the police to get manipulated by him. It was easy for Zayan to show people how everything was still happening on professional terms, and he had not actually promised loyalty to a 'supposed' suspect.

My parents were informed about my decision. They couldn't attend my party because they had travelled out of the city. I informed them about my decision on some non-tracker phone. Mum cried with so much gratitude, pled for me to wait until she returned back. I promised her that I would have a full-family party to celebrate this occasion once I was in the clear.

It hurt a bit how my parents didn't really put any effort to celebrate moments with me, but I was used to this feeling. I had been battling this alone. I knew my parents loved me, adored me...but when a child is constantly causing problems and worries, then even the parents' need a distraction-some diversion.

My dad had stopped attending my calls at night because they made him feel tense. I stopped calling at that time, too.

Anyhow, the party took place in the main house of the farm. Zayan had announced to go clue-hinting with me immediately after the party. We didn't have much time to lose.

People feel happiness, awe-ness at such moments of their lives. All I felt was how terribly lonely it was to start a new chapter of my life solely because of the need to escape from being declared a convict. I was a silent, mute and a defeated host.

Zayan and I sat on a small yellow sofa that had been placed in his garden as our party folded with fervour. The handful of guests at our party invited was served food. People were asked to go inside the kitchen and grab food from the kitchen table. It was a humbling wedding.

"You seem quiet," Zayan spoke, as I mutely kept staring at the ring on my finger gifted to me. Choices...sometimes we have to make extremely tough choices.

"There isn't much to say," I sighed, briefly looking up at him from the corners of my eyes. I couldn't really believe the twist of events.

I was in too much of a trap to experience what it felt like to be the centre of attention, to be treated by a crowd, to be fawned over by my cousins, to go for dress shopping.

"Well, I am just glad that this time no girl called and threatened me to marry her instead." He lowly chuckled with an amused smile, relaxing back into the cushion.

"What do you mean?" I frowned, turning towards him in curiosity.

"Well..." he rubbed the nape of his neck, looking almost a little embarrassed. "Last time, a rumour spread about me being in love, and let's just says the ladies were highly displeased. The phone calls won't stop for nearly a month. I had to get my number changed." He shuddered jokingly at the memory. A thought struck me.

Zayan...he was my partner now. Clearly, he had so many options. This man was rich, powerful and smart. He had options, so why did he choose to stay with someone with so much baggage and issues.

I wasn't the popular girl in college; easily bullied because of my timid and broken personality. The only compliments I had received were from my parents. So many of my relatives claimed that no boy would ever be willing to carry my baggage, so why this man? Why did he look so happy and in awe upon having me sit beside him? I couldn't understand.

"Must have been tough." I allowed a small, joking smile on my face, as he returned my gesture with a smirk.

"I survived." He chuckled, dramatically heaving a sigh. I laughed in amusement.

This man...he was something else.

Leaning so casually against the back of the sofa, draping one arm draped around the sofa and resting on the headrest behind me, he seemed so oddly happy, relaxed, full of pride and so at peace...like he had just won.

"Okay, now let's get someone to serve us food..." He then gestured one roaming helper towards us, with one arm still draped around the back of the sofa-acting like a protective shield behind my back.

"Sure," I shrugged, not really hungry.

Once some food platters got placed on the table before us, we began choosing our selects.

"Oh, just one thing..." Zayan spoke, as he cut a piece of steak and placed it on the plate that was placed before me.

"What?" I took a long sip of soda, eyeing him curiously.

"For our first lunch together...you choose the restaurant."

"Library," I immediately spoke, causing him to narrow his eyebrows in confusion.

"What?"

"We have to solve my case, remember. This has all been to help me out."

Strike one!

Chapter 9

Nyla

17th October...my trials were going to start from 17th October. It was time to get serious. The Embalian Forest Killings had the courts pressured into giving a verdict. One wrong step, and I would easily be convicted on the basis of one simple piece of evidence. I had to be vigilant.

Learning that the creatures feared Zayan was an extremely vital discovery. I had to find the trigger, anything that could finally allow being freed from those deadly clutches because this time if I did get caught, the creatures weren't going to spare me. I had seen the anger. I had to stay close to Zayan.

Sitting at the backside of the library, I skimmed through some books about our town's history while Zayan fished out some old newspapers clipping from the old bookshelves. He wanted to thoroughly explore the types of crimes committed in Embalia, wanted to read about the convicted killers of Embalia. There had to be a pattern.

Zayan claimed that I had to be honest with him, that I had to tell him what was going on. I couldn't. I had been down this road. I didn't want another person, especially my husband, to consider me as an insane person.

I had to fight for my freedom using more realistic ways.

I told Zayan that I had no idea what was going on, which was true. I had no ideas about the creatures stalking me, about what exactly they wanted. So, here we were at the library going through stuff and exploring the criminal history of the town. Though, secretly, I was searching for newspapers that talked about my husband's court cases.

I wanted to know more about this mysterious detective, read how he was described in the newspapers. Something about his past could be extremely crucial and reveal the weak points of the creatures. I had to figure it out.

Zayan had placed two cups of coffee on our table, as we spent hours seeping through newspapers. We have been spared extra hours at the library because the old librarian, apparently, had a soft spot of Zayan.

Having found an old journal that included Embalia's criminal case history, I skimmed through its table of contents and skipped towards the chapters I was looking for.

The Embalia's western court has declared Zayan Khan innocent in the Red Diamond's case.

Splendid!

Young professional horserider was accused of smuggling red diamonds in the city. He and his fiance, who had pled not guilty, were found on the western ports, trading smuggling red diamonds into the city. Though first having accepted the charges and being imprisoned for five years, Zayan defended his case and managed to overturn the charges in his favour. Sherry Khan-the fiance-has proved to be the main culprit behind the smuggling of red diamonds.

Red diamonds...I had heard about those rare jewels found near the upper mountains of Pakistan and Afghanistan. I had been to Pakistan once. The place was exotically abundant in jewels. I remember eating mangoes and meeting friendly Pakistanis who treated my family like royalty. It had been a family trip.

The villagers would tell us about red diamonds found deep in the caves and how greedy foreigners would seep them out of the local's lands. The red diamonds were a rare beauty.

Zayan

Soft eyes so curiously lost in the depth of an old journal. Standing on her right side, Zayan twirled the coffee around in the coffee cup and hid a small smile as she looked so adorable as a detective. Such an innocent and sweet detective.

The criminals had no case.

Not a fair war at all.

Rolling his wedding finger with his thumb, he lowly chuckled as Nyla sighed and rubbed her forehead to keep her brain muscles rolling. She hadn't even touched her coffee mug. Such a pity. She didn't realize that coffee liquid was essential for thinking smart. He did. He momentarily sat on the floor, took a long sip and then got up, knowing that it was time his little wife took a break.

He was going to handle this case. She was fretting over nothing. Now that she had decided to be his, he was going to make sure he got to keep her. He was sincere about his regret, had been smug upon having her fall so easily for his trap. To see her dazzling smile and knowing that he was going to protect it...it made him feel so powerfully possessive and strong. He had been a complete fool when deciding to let this gem go.

The first time he had seen her...he just knew he was never letting her go, that her eyes...her hauntingly captivating eyes...they were going to entrap him into forever fighting for her. He had already judged what moves to make next.

Now, it was time to take his powerful wife out for an evening dining.

"Nyla, why don't we go and grab food from this restaurant-"

"No need. I am not hungry. You can grab a bite and come back here," she quickly spoke, not looking up from the journal.

Scowling in annoyance, with a hint of amusement and frustration almost tipping his expressions into a smile, he pretended to grab her by the shoulders and shake her...only to straighten up and grin charmingly, innocently, when she looked up at him.

"What?" She raised an unamused eyebrow, looking a bit weirded out.

"Nothing. So found something?" He walked towards her, moving to grab the book in her hands. A little too abruptly, she slammed the book shut and looked straight at him-looking almost guilty.

"Why do you live alone? Where are uncle and aunt?" She asked, curiously looking at him. Finally! She wanted to get to know him. She had been secretly reading his case details when all she had to do was ask him. She hadn't really heard much from his parents, family, after he had decided to leave.

"Guilt." He simply shrugged, light and a carefree smile playing on his face, as his emotions remained chill and casual...as if he wasn't bothered by this confession.

"I don't understand-"

"After all that pain I put my pa and ma through-for a woman," an almost sad chuckle escaped. "I didn't really have the guts to stay with them. I was a wealthy man. My parents moved to Turkey. I chose to stay behind" He revealed, taking a seat next to Nyla. Her expressions softened at this confession.

"You are a fool if you let guilt come in the way of being with your family. Trust me, what I would do to be beside my family, but alas, I can't." She leaned a bit back, a sweetened and rueful smile on her face; even though, her expressions showed hurt.

He smiled. "Well, I do have to visit my parents soon. I have to thank them for choosing you for me" He beamed, showing his teeth, staring deep into her gaze.

For a moment, her expressions turned tender, like her heart had been softened by such a confession, but she quickly looked away, tucking a lock of hair behind her hair.

Zayan could see that she was saving herself, shielding herself. Emotions...this girl had got hurt because of that, but how could he tell her that his heartbeat, soul beamed in her presence...that his senses turned so fresh and uplifting when she smiled at him. How could he tell her that her emotions were controlling his...

With a small smile appearing on his face, he simply shook his head and began helping her out in profiling her court case.

One step at a time...he would heal her heart.

He just needed to know why she was lying about not knowing anything about the reasons behind the murders.

Chapter 10

Z ayan

She was silent. Her eerie quirks, her cautiousness, and then there was that fear in her eyes when she had been escorted to the forest and quietly waited…it was an odd case of a mysterious reality.

What could be sinister enough to make her lie?

Strange humans….hmmm

For a long time, her truth hadn't been believed, her insanity had been questioned, so it made sense for her to speak limited words. Yet she had married him because she believed that he had heard her truth. Why then was she still lying? She wanted him to fight. She wasn't displaying the vulnerabilities, which hardly made any sense.

Sitting in the lounge of the police station, Zayan rolled the edges of the book pages, while leaning back on his chair, and patted his chin in deep thought. Nyla was sitting before him, right across the huge table placed between them, with her head resting against one open journal. She was fast asleep, snoring and muttering something about not leaving her alone and not turning off the lights.

A gentle smile appeared on Zayan's smile, as he saw her then adorably scolding someone in her sleep and demanding for her favourite stuffed pink lilies cushion. This woman was adorable. The strong feeling of possessive made him curl his fists in a solid promise. This was his woman.

It was hard to believe that such a gentle and adorable soul was being accused of something as sinister as committing murders, slashing heads and clawing people. Yet, how could one use her sweet vibe as a piece of evidence?

Randomly cracking his knuckles, Zayan rubbed the nape of his nape and then stared up at the ceiling. He was feeling bored now. His mind, it could hardly remain steadfast on one track. He had an idea of what he was going to say at the opening hearing...what evidences he was going to provide. It was the lack of answers that were boring his mind.

The mystery was still the same. What was happening to Embalian people deep in the forest? Why Nyla was always coincidentally there? And why were so many of those people whom she knew being targetted?

What was Mrs Zayan hiding from her dear husband?

17th October...

Time: 9: 00 am

Court Case: Embalian Forest Killings

Coverage: The Embalian Grand Newspaper, Twin news articles, Lily Gardens journals and That Embalian Police's National Journal.

Nyla

I was terrified, trying my best to control my tangled nerves. The hearing was about to begin at any time soon. It felt so agonizing to be sitting as a suspect and watching a wave of crowd notice my each and every move. Any wrong move of mine could be used as evidence against me.

I could feel it in the air-the atmosphere. Many already accepted me guilty. It was one of those cases that the obvious picture was easily used by the witnesses. I understood the reasoning behind such assumptions. The hurt was too huge for anyone to think rationally.

Fidgeting with my fingers, I turned to look at the prosecution side of the court and sighed in deep pain. There were innocent and so deeply hurt families waiting there, hoping that Mr Jaffar-the city's prime lawyer- could help them receive justice. All of the wounded families were bonding over their mutual pain.

I turned to momentarily look at the alien-crowd sitting behind me. No one from my family was attending this court hearing. My mama didn't have the heart to see me in such a horrible mess.

Taking deep breaths, I watched Zayan who was standing so tall and powerful before me. He momentarily turned around to give me a charming grin and winked playfully in assurance, and then with an obvious show of confidence, he turned back and waited for the judge to start the hearing. It was obvious by my husband's stance that he was in control.

The women in the jury seemed on my side.

I could feel the attention...the desperation to remain unbiased.

Everyone seemed curious and charmed in the presence of a young charming lawyer. There were also so many eyes that were gazing in my direction. My heart was aching because these lurking gazes were so desperate for justice that they were prayed for me to be labelled guilty.

Soon, my case hearing began. The judge started reading the case file; the accusations made against me. I had pled non-guilty, so now both the prosecution and the defence had to state their opening statements.

The prosecution was to begin first.

Mr Jaffar stood up and walked before the judge's desk, gaining momentum to address both the judge and the crowd. He stated the accusations registered against me, stated the demand of the prosecution.

Mr Jaffar seemed so cold and spoke with hidden malice as he referred to be being the prime suspect. The accusations almost made me want to wince and hideaway. They made me feel so tiny. I looked towards Zayan in worry and watched him standing with a patient and completely calm stance, rocking subtly on his foot heels. I breathed in deeply. My husband seemed confident.

We could do this.

Once the prosecution had stated their opening statement, Zayan started stating my side of the case. The crowd literally melted into charmed silence, as they seemingly captivated by the butter-like words spoken by my husband.

'Your honor, I would now like to invite my first witness to the stand." Zayan then asked for permission. I was confused about this. Who was he going to call?

Fidgeting with my fingers, I watched curiously and held my breath as the courtroom doors opened. Whom could Zayan had chosen as a witness?

'Mr Emir Junaid. His sister 'Nadia' was murdered in the forest." Zayan introduced. Nadia's brother was here? I felt so ashamed.

I kept my eyes lowered as Emir made it to the witness stand, and Zayan walked towards him.

"Mr Emir, were you close to your sister?" Zayan questioned.

"Ummm...she was, still is, my best friend. I miss her so much." The boy's voice wobbled. I felt terrible.

"What kind of sister was in college? Did she have any preferences in the type of friends she made?"

"Objection, your honour. Any personal details that aren't relevant to the case are to be left out." Mr Jaffar immediately stood up.

"These are quite relevant since my client has experienced being an easy target of torment in college. One of the rumoured tormentors was Miss Nadia."

What the heck!

What was Zayan doing? By stating this, he had made me sound even more of a suspect. I didn't like it when people got to know about my experience of bullying. I didn't like being pitied, treated inferior and being reminded of moments that hurt.

Mentioning this information had just boasted the prosecution's energy. The audience supporting the wounded families had turned smug and interested in this news. A subtle chuckle even echoed. Zayan had given them more substance to hold on. They were thinking that this man was only words, not much about brains.

However, instead of looking like he had spilt out wrong words, Zayan was standing confidently, not even bothered by the change in the atmosphere.

The judge simply slammed his wooden hammer.

"Objection overruled." He stated.

"Good. So, as I was saying, Mr Emir. Your sister used to torment Miss Nadia. She was murdered in the same forest visited on a daily basis by Nyla. Is that correct?"

"Umm...yeah," Emir spoke awkwardly, seeming sounding in too much pain to talk about this.

"Yet, when the statement you recorded in the police station showed that you harboured no ill-notions for Nyla and claimed that she was innocent. Is that right?" Zayan spoke.

"Right."

"Here is the recorded statement printed out in the form of a hardcopy." He then submitted a file to the judge.

The atmosphere shifted again.

Zayan had just shown that a man who had claimed to love his sister had called me innocent. He could claim that I had a motive, some rooting, but he didn't.

A remarkable move by Zayan.

"Why is that?" He then continued with the interrogation.

"Miss Nyla is a nice person. She never hurt anyone." The awkward shyness was there. I blushed too. This was insane.

Nadia's brother...he liked me.

"I see. Mrs Nyla is a nice person. That will be all for now." The light ting of coldness was there in Zayan's tone, but this confession was vital to hear. One of the people who had lost a loved one was siding with me. This was huge.

Fortunately, the crowd seemed to forgo the replacement of Miss and Mrs. It was either Zayan's charm, confidence that no one interrupted or questioned that mistake, or simply something that was seen as a human error.

After Emir left the witness stand, the prosecution brought a few of their own witness, provided the matching-paint as evidence. It was just a routine process, and the court hearing was then adjourned. The next hearing was to take place on 29th October.

"That was surprising," I spoke, as I walked alongside Zayan to his car.

"I told you that I would take care of it."

"Yeah...and the court was so oddly biased when it came to you." I pointed.

After the hearing, one of the elderly woman sitting in the crowd had even told Zayan that her granddaughter was looking for a good proposal, and Zayan could be the one for her. Zayan had only chuckled at such an offer like he was used to such attention.

"Jealous..." he teased, showing me his pearly whites.

"Seriously?" I narrowed my eyebrows and frowned. There was so much going on. I didn't really time for such normal emotions.

"Never mind." He simply smiled, shaking his head and opened the door of his McLaren car.

"Oh, and Emir's confession was embarrassing," I continued, sitting in the passenger seat. The atmosphere of the court, it had provoked my talkative mood. The adrenaline rush had me wanting to discuss what had happened.

"I loved the Mrs part..." He met my gaze with a playful grin. I blushed again.

"Umm...so what will happen next?" I changed the topic.

"We will see." Confident, he reversed the car with one hand on the steering wheel and then drove us down the open roads of Embalia.

We will see.

Chapter 11

Z ayan

 She was eating a slice of chocolate cake, enjoying the chocolate goodness with a smile on her face. Simply snacking on a packet of chips, Zayan watched with curiosity as she pushed the chocolate chip topping aside and eat the sponge first. She was leaving the best part for later. Sweet.

Eating one chip at a time, Zayan was sitting on a brown couch with one arm lazily plopped on the couch's arm while Nyla sat on the sofa that was placed before him, right across the room. They were in the police quarter and enjoying an evening meal. The court hearing had gone well. It was time to relax and enjoy some food. Yet, Zayan couldn't help but attentively observe his wife's mannerism. She seemed too relaxed, sort of like freed.

Hmmm…

"You don't mind not having white lights switched on," he spoke after a minute, silently taking chewing on another chip. His eyes fully focused on his wife.

"What?" She looked up at him confused, taking a spoonful of her chocolate cake.

"The white lights...they used to be your demand when staying in the prison cell, along with wanting some company. You don't demand such strange things now." He noticed, leaned back. His gaze sharp and alert.

For a moment, she looked nervous...averting her gaze towards the plate. "Umm...I don't need them anymore."

"Why?" He raised an eyebrow, yet again eating another chip. It was like enjoying a good book...being an audience to someone's story.

"I-I feel safe with you." She blushed. Her voice so adorably sweet and shy, that Zayan didn't care about how she was still not telling the complete truth. This woman knew how to destroy a man's heart, ruin his life.

"Good." He simply remarked with a proud smirk.

"How come you are so good at being a lawyer, yet you work as a detective?" she then spoke, probably changing the topic. Zayan smiled at such a sweetly naive question.

"Being a lawyer was my need when I was imprisoned. I enjoy looking for a case before I defend it." He beamed, his pearly whites shining as he spoke about his passions. He was a bored man, and mysteries intrigued him.

Nyla's gaze was one of the most mysterious depths of beauty he had ever seen. He liked gazing into them and picking on her emotions. She was an extremely emotional person.

"Yet you have momentarily taken a break from your detective work to help me out." She pointed.

"Did I tell you that I am also madly obsessed with protecting my family, my girl? You ladies are one of my main weaknesses." He teased, earning another blush from her.

"You are just-"

"Sweet and protective?" He added with a grin before she could finish. "I know." He nodded, without letting her answer.

Crushing his chip packet into a ball, he then got up and ruffled his hair. "Little doe, I have some work to do. I will be leaving my mobile at home because technology...ugh" he shuddered with exaggerated disgust, hiding a smile and holding in a playful chuckle. "But don't worry. I will be returning back in a couple of hours. Then we can head to your favourite spot-the library." He joked.

"W-What time?" She suddenly asked, sounding nervous and a little scared.

"Twelve, my little doe. Don't worry."

"Umm...o-okay." She began fidgeting with her fingers.

Knowing that she would be fine, Zayan stepped out of the quarter. He had some investigation to do...some little research. Tonight, he was going to enjoy a blazing hot cup of coffee deep in the eerie forest.

Nyla

He left.

Assuring me that he would return, promising that we would continue researching on my case once he returned back, he left. I gulped in nervousness. His presence scared the creatures. They hadn't managed to come near me. They were staying away from my quarters because Zayan was there to help me look for vital pieces of evidence that would support my case.

It was eerie and dreadful. With sweat brimming my forehead, I sat in the living room alone. The clock ticks were haunting me. They would saw up again. Those furious creatures...with Zayan not available at the time they loved to attack...I wouldn't be spared.

I had to do something.

I shouldn't have let Zayan leave.

Gulping, with my nails digging deep into the palm of my hands, I looked at the glistening sight of twilight shining outside my window.

No...No...No...

Suddenly, I heard a crackling sound of childish laughter echoing from outside my window. It was too innocent, too carefree and too excited. Shoot! They were here, already. This had never happened before.

They were here.

Snapping my head towards the window, I felt all colours draining out of my face as I found them staring at me. They had their faces and hands pressed against the glass window. The maniac wide grins were there on their face, and their blank-expressionless-eyes were looking insanely happy now.

They seemed to be waiting impatiently, their claws lightly tapping against the glass. I felt faint. The look in their eyes...it was the same look when they hunted. Yet it seemed more eager now.

Shoot!

Frantic, I got up. It wasn't the time. They were waiting. I had to find Zayan. H-He...I had to get to him. Grabbing a rolling pin from the little kitchen, I headed out. Knives...I didn't dare use them against these creatures. I had no idea where Zayan was. I had to head to the police station.

People...I needed them.

My heart was racing fast. Just taking one step out of the quarter had me frantic and terrified. I was in the open now-so like prey. I had to run.

Not even daring to blink, I rushed out of my quarter and headed towards the fields. I had to make a run for it. Tears were rolling down my cheeks as I hurried past the grass. No one was around. I heard cackling shrieks and the sound of laughter echoing in the air.

Oh no!

Claws dug in the ground and nails rubbed against the floor in a predatory manner. I couldn't help but shriek this time. I had been such a fool to not convince Zayan to stay. I just didn't want him to be suspicious. He was smart. I didn't want him to think that I was mentally struggling, to stop defending case, yet sounding like a fool seemed better than being hunted.

I don't know what I was thinking when I had allowed Zayan to leave.

"What is going on?" There was a policeman patrolling this area.

Poor man!

There were probably cameras installed in this area and wire bars acting as fields, so one guard enough for patrolling. Yet the police had no idea that the creatures attacked were swift and hardly captured by cameras.

The police officer was near. He had started rushing after me. Yet, he was only near to me. He sounded nearer to the creatures. With deep pain, I had to keep running while that man, unknowingly, took the creatures' attention away from me.

The sound of a tortured cry followed by the slashing sound of flesh being torn apart echoed in the air, as I ran away from the crime scene. The police officer only got a minute to beg for help before he was ambushed by the creatures.

I didn't even bother to look back and headed straight to the police station. Tears were rushing down my cheeks. There were only a few officers on duty at this time. I noticed one who was familiar.

"Officer Bahadur," I ran up to him. All attention was on me now.

"What's wrong?" He sounded alert and concerned, noticing my terrified and frantic stance...the rolling pin in my hand.

"Zayan...I need to know where he is." I spoke in a hurry, huffing and working hard to inhale air.

"Asher! Asher is lying dead in the fields." Immediately one police barged into the station.

"What happened?" This time, Bahadur narrowed his eyes at me; his expressions stern, strict and firm. I gulped.

Shoot!

CHAPTER 12

N yla

I shivered and trembled. Thick tears were running down my cheeks, as I pulled on locks of my hair in agony. This was a mess...a huge mess. My heart was beating fast. Immediately after Asher's death, I had been arrested...taken into custody for the rest of my court hearings.

I was a mess.

"Seriously, what the heck! What happened?" Outside, I saw Zayan finally making his way towards my prison. He looked extremely furious and stressed out-nothing like the calm and charming guy I had known him to be.

Several police officers were following him, as he stomped to my prison and grabbed the prison bars.

"Seriously, Nyla, what happened? Do you know they just rejected your bail? Tell me what happened? What did you do to that guard?" He fumed, his temper seemingly unable to hide his concerns and fear. I could see that he didn't like me behind the bars.

"Sir-"

"I would like a moment with my client!" He snapped at the officers standing behind him, causing them to immediately mutter a quick 'okay' and rush back to their positions.

Zayan was a person who smiled and laughed. Seeing his angry side made me shiver. He seemed terrifying when in a foul mood. Maybe that is the reason why he tended to laugh and joke around. His temper was just too terrifying and scary...reminded me how I felt around the creatures.

"What happened, Nyla?" His stern gaze was back on me, making me breathe hitch as another sob arose. I was sitting on a bench that was pressed against the left wall of the prison. One of my hands was curled around the seat, squeezing the steel for comfort.

"I-I-I-"

"The CCTV showed Asher rushing after you when he suddenly collapsed on the floor and the cameras stopped working, so tell me what did you do?" His voice reached octaves, as my cry grew louder.

"I-I didn't do anything." I got up, my eyes staring at him so desperately, my stance seeming so petrified. "Y-You have to believe me. I-I didn't kill that guard." I rushed up to hold the bars, too...my gaze so earnestly wishing for him to believe.

He kept staring at me with a stoic expression, silently observing the tears rolling down my cheek, and then looked to his right while heaving a deep sigh and ruffling his hair. His stiff stance turned soft.

"So what happened when I left?" He turned to look at me again, wiping my flowing tears with the back of his hands. I was so desperately wanting him to believe me; my soul so wounded and alone. I felt so tiny and dishevelled.

"I-I got scared and decided to look for you." I stared deep into his eyes, waiting for him to believe me. If he didn't, I don't know what I was going to do.

"What happened to Asher?"

"I-I don't know. You have to believe me. I-I have no idea what is going on. Please!"

"Nyla-" His stance looked hesitant thoughtful.

"Please don't give up on me." I sobbed, tears rolling down my cheeks against. I curled my fist around his. "I know this seems extremely suspicious, but I-I am telling you that I didn't kill that man. You have to believe me. I can't stay here alone at night. I am scared. I am begging you...please don't leave me all alone. I won't be able to bear that. I need you!" I was hyperventilating now; my breaths coming in short intervals.

I couldn't be alone. Zayan had to stay. The creatures would get me. They would get me. I had to leave. I had to do something. I couldn't stay in this place. The walls were suffocating me.

"Shh...calm down. It is okay. I believe you..hush..." Zayan now tenderly began removing my hand that had made its way to the locks of my hair and was pulling on it in maniac stress. I was almost feeling faint with fear.

"Relax...it is okay..." He continued cooing and assuring that everything was going to alright until I finally calmed down. My breaths remained unsteady, yet I managed to control my emotions. I almost felt ashamed for breaking down like this in front of Zayan, but I really needed him here.

"I will come to visit you every night and leave at dawn. If that fine?" He asked tenderly, once I had turned completely calm and was feeling quiet.

"Okay. I would like that." I muttered in a tiny and weak tone. He gave me a soft smile.

"You are cheating! Play fair. I don't like pity wins." I scowled with a childish nag in my tone, watching as Zayan simply shrugged and put his red token back in its original place.

"Your eyes were distracting me." He cheekily spoke.

"They weren't distracting you when we first started playing this game..." I was acting a child, but this was something I really missed. I didn't get to have many friends, stayed away from other children, so I wanted to act like a child, let go of my demons and act silly, irrational and carefree for once.

"They were. I just wanted to impress you." He charmed, making me huff and shake my head.

It was late at night.

Both of us were playing Ludo. Zayan was sitting on the floor, right in front of my prison, and I was sitting on my folding legs. before him, with the prison barriers enacting as a barrier between us. Both of us had decided to pass the time playing a fun game.

I suggested playing Ludo.

However, having lost three games of Ludo in a row, I knew that Zayan was taking pity on me the fourth time we played the game. All my green tokens were at home, while 3 of his had already made it to the winning point. He was purposely making sure that his fourth token didn't reach the winning spot.

"You know I have never felt so bad at winning a game before," Zayan then casually leaned back, resting on one and chuckling a little as he eyed me thinking of the best plan to defeat him.

"How are you so good at this game?" I whined, finally giving up, wondering why the heck I wasn't getting the darn six. The dice seemed to be rigged in Zayan's favour.

"I solve crimes. Planning strategies isn't something new to me. Also, I am quite skilled when it comes to fooling my opponents." He gave me a wide mischievous grin. My eyes widened in realization.

"Wait! You have been cheating?"

"I call it planning a strategy." He spoke, looking highly amused by my shocked reaction.

"What the heck! How?" I frowned. I couldn't understand how he had managed to cheat. I had been quite attentive when playing this game.

"You are adorably naive. It is not really hard." He shrugged. "I just rolled the dice in a manner that I would get sixes."

What the heck!

How did he manage to do that?

"How?" I couldn't help but ask.

"Practice. I used to play this game with my 2-year-old niece when she would want to play. Little children really love playing this game," he spoke with a smirk.

Har, Har!

He was teasing me for suggesting such a childish game, but I couldn't help it. I used to play this game with my grandmother. Playing this game just made me feel warm.

Simply smiling and shaking my head at him, I eyed the clock hanging in my prison and took a deep breath. The creatures hadn't shown up. It was past their time to show up. A relieved smile appeared on my face and I folded my hands...feeling the weight on my shoulders get lifted off.

"You know..." Zayan spoke matter of factly, his sharp gaze meeting mine, as he folded his hands before his-leaning in my direction.

"If you weren't so adorably sweet and seemed so innocent, I would have definitely considered you as an obvious suspect."

"I-I-"

"But you are adorably sweet and have such an innocent vibe." He rested on his arms again. "So I won't consider you a suspect even if you stab my heart. You are already holding it. Who knows when my little wife will squeeze it." He chuckled. I gulped in discomfort.

"Ummm, Z-Zayan-"

"I will take care of this case, Nyla." He assured, giving me a tender look. "I know what has happened to Asher has complicated things, but you are my responsibility. I believe you. I will get my wife out of this mess. I will respect your choice of not sharing your fears with me. I won't leave you."

Tears of emotions started rolling down my eyes. Even when my family had given up on me, this man was claiming to take a stand for me. I-I had been so wrong about Zayan. He wasn't an overly frank and irritating guy. He was a man with a genuinely good heart.

I smiled through my tears. "Thank you." My voice was low, as I lowered my gaze towards my fidgeting fingers. My heartbeat had picked up a fast pace.

CHAPTER 13

2 9th October 2019

Court Case: Embalian Forest Killings

Coverage: The Embalian Grand Newspaper, Twin news articles, Lily Gardens journals and That Embalian Police's National Journal.

Nyla

Zayan's fists were curled. There was an underlined frown on his face, and I could see him resisting the urge to clench his jaws. Momentary happiness of Zayan staying with my side and the creatures not showing up had distracted me, but now it was back to a dire reality.

Asher's death had literally damaged my case.

Mr Jaffar was brutally slaughtering the proof of my innocence before the court. Videos had been provided. My own mother's retelling of how I used to kill cats when little had been given as a piece of evidence. That little bit had really broken my heart. I remembered that day...it was traumatizing.

But I don't blame my mother for sharing moments of my past. She had to do the right thing. My demons weren't easy to register. My medical case files had been brought forward.

My mental state was so questionable.

Currently, the owner of the mental asylum I used to stay at was being questioned by the prosecution. The woman was spitting garbage about my sanity. Zayan had stood up to object, state that the prosecution was leading the witness, but alas...there was so much proof.

I wanted to pull on locks of my hair and scream that I wasn't insane. I wasn't silly, hurt and a murderer. I was scared-just so terribly scared.

Chewing on my thumbnail in anxiety and nervousness, I eyed Zayan with a teary and mute expression, hurting over how harshly I was being accused of such sinister crimes. I actually felt quite embarrassed to have my issues displayed so publically. I used to feel annoyed by this annoyingly frank detective sitting next to me, but now, with him as my husband, I didn't like my image being tarnished. I felt ashamed.

The audience was watching in silence. So many families were waiting for the verdict...already considering me as guilty. I could feel the anger, the pain....it made me feel so suffocated in this atmosphere-so hurt and alone.

After Mr Jaffar had presented the case, I nervously watched as Zayan got up to address the prosecutions' witness.

"Your honour, I would like to ask some questions from Doctor Haya." His powerful stance was quick to demand control over the courtroom's environment. The lady stenographer stopped typing for a minute. The judge nodded.

Folding his arms behind his back, Zayan began pacing before the witness stand...his stance showing no hint of humour. He was so ridiculously confident and charming that I felt intimidated on the behalf of Doctor Haya. My husband was one dangerous man. I had been taking him lightly, being so straight-forward when he was offering me charming and sweet smiles. I needed to be more appreciative of his humorous side.

"You have confessed to one of your doctors being fired on the basis of temper issues, and you have claimed that Nyla was a complicated case. Is that true?" He questioned; though, it was obvious that he just wanted her to agree.

"Y-Yes." The woman seemed to be working too hard to keep up the act of being unaffected and unintimidated. She had her hands folded and her voice in control. I remember seeing her once or twice during some counselling sessions, yet I didn't hate her.

Doctor Sana...she was the woman who had been so ruthless with my case.

"Okay. Does your institute record or supervise the sessions you have with your patients?" Zayan sharply asked.

"No." She shook her head. "We respect the privacy of our patients. We don't indulge in acts that can-"

"But how do you monitor your new employees' performance if you don't supervise them?" Zayan mused with fake curiosity. A moment of hesitation followed after.

"Objection, your honour!" The prosecution's lawyer stood up, making me subtly frown in annoyance. I felt like Zayan was on to something. Some women sitting behind me also didn't like the prosecution's interference.

"This is a case of leading the witness!" Mr Jaffar pointed.

"Overruled." The judge simply ordered and gestured for Zayan to continue again.

Composed, Zayan simply nodded with a serious expression on his face while showing no signs of irritation and annoyance. He was giving the prosecution the time to speak, bring all pieces of evidence because it felt like he had a plan.

"As I was saying," he continued with a bored tone, making Mr Jaffar's interruption seem merely unimportant and time-wasting. "You don't supervise your employees. You fire your employees on the basis of complaints you get, and one of Nyla's medical reports show that she often had nail marks on her hands. They were noticed once when she returned back from her meeting with your doctor. Is that true?" He asked Doctor Haya.

"Yes. Her parents were actually worried about her getting so bruised easily." She explained.

A deep sense of nostalgic pain had me lowering my gaze and looking at my hands.

My mama would ask me about the scratches on my hands, scold me for being so clumsy, yet I couldn't convince her that I had nothing to do with the battle scars on my hands. Doctor Sana would call me clumsy, too.

I wondered where Zayan was going with this.

"Hmm." I looked up again as he hmmed in deep thought. The interrogation was hurting my heart. I felt horrible how everyone was talking about me. I felt low and defeated just by the thought of how much misery those creatures had caused me.

Zayan had stopped to pinch his chin in a distracted manner.

"Doctor Haya, given what you have told me, is there a chance if bias results if the victim is too little or too complicated to speak up against ill-treatment?" He turned in the doctor's direction.

"We are very thorough in our policies about bullying." She started explaining again. "We regulate them. All the sessions are noted down and submitted to the main office. We conduct workshops and do make the employees give weekly demos in front of our heads."

"By the doctors who conducted those sessions?" Zayan quickly pointed- a hint of knowing smile appearing in his tone.

"Yes."

"I see." He began pacing in front of her stand again, one hand ruffling his hair while the other folded behind his back. The subtle grin on his face was showing that he had lured Doctor Haya directly into his trap. This had me furrow my brows and listen.

"So, Doctor Haya, is it a possibility that Doctor Sana could have made a mistake when conducting her sessions?" A hint of a knowing smirk appeared in his tone.

"Objection, your honour!" Mr Jaffar was at it again.

Completely ignoring Mr Jaffar, Zayan made his way towards the stand again and bite on his thumbnail. "Your institution has declared Nyla to be mentally unstable. But what you just revealed shows that your medical reports have no credibility. You have depended on one person's report despite the fact that you have to fire an employee because of complaints about their temper issues. So, Doctor Haya, I ask again...is it possible for your institute to have conducted an error when dealing with Nyla's case?" He persisted with sharpness and clever intimidation.

"Our doctors don't have any motives to do so." Her voice sounded timid.

"True." He accepted with a nod. "Yet I have Doctor Sana's bank statements that show Doctor Sana used to suffer from budget constraints and was in dire need for economic funds to maintain living all alone in the city before she got employed at your institute.

Nyla's case has always a complicated one, and her parents were paying a heavy fee for her to get diagnosed with something that would make sense. The stories shared by Nyla's mother show that her mother was looking for a complex and an appropriate answer-one that was given by Doctor Sana."

"Objection, your honour!" Mr Jaffar stood up immediately. "Is Mr Zayan stating facts or opinion?"

A tiny smirk appeared on Zayan's face. He has a smile edging close as he turned towards Mr Jaffar and beamed.

"All facts."

"Your honour," he then submitted a file to the judge with a smug look on his face. "Here is the bank statement of Doctor Sana, along with her work experience letter.

The reports show how Doctor Haya allowed Doctor Sana, who had just one year's experience, to work independently with such a complicated case. It shows an act of negligence and a chance of medical reports to get easily manipulated. Also, it threatens to create a false image of a person."

Oh, the realization began sinking in.

My eyes widened with surprise. I looked around the court, noticing the same expression. Everyone looked surprised...almost impressed.

By proving that I might be incorrectly diagnosed, Zayan had pointed out how this mistake can create a false image of mine in other's hands: therefore, making it more convenient for others to blame me for the crimes I didn't commit.

"Your Honour, I would next like to call Sheriff Bahadur on the stand, please..." Zayan then announced. Doctor Haya almost looked ashamed when walking away from the stands. She had been spitting so many terrible facts about me. Now she felt how it was to be humiliated in public. I watched her walk away with pity and understanding.

My attention went back to Zayan as Doctor Haya took her seat.

This was like a catalyst.

Zayan had set the mood. Now it was time to prove how I couldn't be linked to the killing cases. Hope had been ignited. I was intrigued to know how this man was going to do so.

Leaning forward on my seat, like so many others around me, I listened as Sheriff Bahadur was asked to stand on the witness stand.

"Sheriff Bahadur, you have had been assisting on helping me solve this case. Right?" Zayan began interrogating.

"Yep, Sir," Bahadur spoke with pride. This is how Northern men were. They held pride in being able to serve their country.

"Have you noticed the 'claw' marks mostly found on the victims'?"

"Yes, Sir."

"Were those marks on Asher-the policeman who recently got murdered?" He confirmed.

"Yes." There was no accusation, no hostility in Bahadur's tone. It felt like that this man wasn't randomly holding a grudge against me. I felt guilty about how gentle some people were being about my hidden secrets.

"So, given the timeframe when Asher got 'supposedly' murdered, Nyla had to be holding onto something sharp to make those marks. Right?" Zayan then suggested. I think I was beginning to catch a gist of where he was going with this.

I listened with sole attentiveness.

"Yes, Sir."

"Was she holding something at that time?" He raised an eyebrow, frankly placing an elbow on the stand.

"Umm...she was holding a rolling pin." Bahadur sounded a bit nervous.

"Any signs of blood?"

"Umm...none. She looked scared and terrified."

"With no sharp weapon in her hand, do you believe Nyla would have time to hide the murder weapon after committing the murder?" Zayan sounded nonchalant, yet I knew that he was silently luring another victim into his trap.

Brilliant!

The scenario suddenly turned eager and intense.

"No, Sir," Bahadur immediately shook his head. "The police even searched the premises, so there is no way that Madam Nyla could be able to hide anything given the short timeframe in which the murder took place."

"Yet, the police found the trace of paint that belongs to Nyla's baseball bat on one of the victim's head. Right?" Zayan gave the evidence himself, making me frown.

Huh?

"Yes, Sir," Bahadur replied sombrely.

"Well...Bahadur, my northern brother," Zayan began pacing ...a small smile again on his face. This man was super strange and unpredictable. What was he planning to say now?

"According to the medical reports of that victim, he died because of the scars on him and not because of the blow on his head. So do you think it is possible that Nyla has been actually telling the truth, and that there have been animal attacks, which have caused those killings? Also, do you think it is a possibility that the use of a baseball bat by Nyla was in fact an attempt of hers to help the victims?" He stopped and turned to look at Bahadur away. All traces of flexibility and feigned curiosity are gone.

Gasps echoed around the room.

Wow!

I sat up straight in my seat, clutching the table firmly in my hands, as I looked at my husband with so much joy. This was impressive.

"Objection, Your Honour! This is leading the witness!" The prosecution had got into action again.

"Do you?" Zayan repeated; his command so power and firm. He completely ignored the fumed prosecution and the sudden uproar of emotions in the court.

"I do." With a deep sigh, Bahadur admitted in a low tone.

I couldn't believe it.

A happy and wide smile appeared on my face. This was so amazing.

"No further questions, your honour," Zayan spoke satisfied.

The entire court was watching in shock.

With just two witnesses, Zayan had proven that I might not be insane and made one of the police officers admit that I might be innocent. I felt like jumping in my seat in celebration. Though, as I turned to look at the suffering families...my sense of celebration dimmed a bit. These people needed answers. Me being innocent or not really didn't matter to them because their hearts had been broken. There was a high chance that their hearts would never head again.

I looked back at Zayan again, feeling my mood turn so dull and blue, and saw him now walking back towards our table. I gave him a tiny grateful smile, having learned the important lesson of that my husband was not really a man to be trifled with. I shouldn't be taking him so lightly.

Seeing my shy and impressed smile, he mischievously winked with a show of humour.

This man...he had me shaking my head and hiding a grin.

This day had been wonderful.

CHAPTER 14

N^{yla}

The air was breezy and shifting. I was sitting in my prison and drinking a warm cup of hot cocoa. Zayan was drinking his cup of coffee. His mood...it was silently good and sombre. However, the element of humour was sitting from his stance. I had asked him if I would soon be freed, and he had simply shaken his head with a pitiful smile.

"Not quite." He took a sip of coffee and stared straight, while I sat on his left side-bars and listened with a frown. I pressed my hands against the floor to hear him better.

"This is all circumstantial." He turned his head towards me and met my gaze. "I presented a circumstantial scenario. There were so many ifs. If the medical reports were incorrect..." He placed his cup of coffee and fully turned towards me, folding his hands with a sad smile on his face. Zayan being all serious and mature...it was a worrying sight.

"If you don't have an accomplice if you weren't fast enoug h...too many what-ifs. Also, I heard the prosecution is going to bring the head of the forest department who will explain how the scars are caused by any animal's attack. You always being there is going to be used as a catalyst. And Asher's death...you were the only one near. So, as I said...we still have some work to do." He gave me a sad smile, watching as I folded my hands around the bars in tension and focus...my eyes attentively watching

"What am I going to do?" My eyes watered, as I looked at him with an earnest and vulnerable expression, feeling so alone and scared.

I-I didn't do it. It was the creatures. I-I am innocent. Zayan s-said he would take care of me.

"We are going to start with the truth." He wrapped his hands around mine. "You have to tell me exactly the whole truth. I know something abnormal is happening. I know you are scared...but you have to tell me what." He encouraged, his voice so tender and coaxing...eyes staring so deep into mine, wishing for me to share. But I couldn't. Not when I was already trapped in a corner.

He would consider me insane, lost and a murderer. My own family had believed my truth I couldn't risk losing my husband when he was the one trusting me-making me feel normal, scaring the creatures away.

"I-I-"

"Nyla, Don't worry," he softly wiped a rolling tear away from my cheek. "I promised I will take care of you. I won't ever leave you. Even if you decide not to tell me the truth, I will stay. But, my little doe with eyes that will be my ruination, I just want you to trust me. Can you do that?" He muttered with a low chuckle, making me crack a smile too.

"I-I can try," I shyly lowered my gaze to the floor.

"Good. Now I want to talk about how offended I am that you decided to drink hot cocoa instead. Once we get you out of here, you are going to brew coffee for us, and then we are finally going to enjoy our coffee on our vacation house's roof. You still haven't been to my favourite restaurant with me, so-"

"Detective Zayan!" A police officer now came rushing in the direction of our prison. "We found the accomplice. The triple z killer is involved in this. We found him!"

"What the heck!" Zayan immediately stood up.

Triple Z Killer? I didn't have any human accomplice. What on earth was going on! The feeling of dread and fear grew intense, as I curiously listened.

Who had been caught by these people?

"Explain." Zayan simply ordered, causing the man to nod in obedience.

"One of our security guards was caught attacking another man. He was carving scars. We took out his information file and found out that he has been working with an alias. He confessed to being the Triple Z killer who is infamous in

Seenia Island for being a serial killer who hunts humans, leaves them on the floor and enjoys having people around to check out his hard work. He fled from Seenia Island last year. That would explain how our security cameras stopped working. It was him." The man spoke in a rushed manner. I couldn't help but gasp in astonishment.

What an uncanny coincidence!

A serial killer who killed in a similar pattern as found in the Embalian Forest killing had just been caught. The police were thinking he was my accomplice, but he wasn't. He was going to take the blame for the crimes committed by the creatures.

"But how can I be his accomplice when he has already been committing crimes in Seenia Island?" I stood up, too...wanting to clear my name.

"You have claimed there were animal attacks." The police officer turned towards me with sharpness and accusation.

"I-I-"

"That will be all, Zubair." Zayan simply interrupted in a rather cool and composed tone. I looked at him with slight hurt and confusion. The officer simply nodded and headed out. It was strange how people weren't really questioning Zayan spending so much time with me, for being so frank and friendly. Maybe it was the norm.

A pang of discomfort hit me.

"Zayan, why didn't you defend me?" I began complaining once the police officer left. My soul was beating with frustration, the heat of anger making me feel so annoyed. Why didn't Zayan say anything to the officer!

"The court is the place we will defend our case, bella. Not here. There is no point saying this to a low-rank officer." He cooed. working to cool my temper by gently grabbing my hand.

I sighed and then smiled softly. "So is this it? Am I finally going to get out?" I looked at him with a tender expression. My soul felt elated..giddy. I felt like jumping with joy. I couldn't believe the twist in events. Such luck...I felt bad for having someoneelse being accused of my crimes, but that someone was a serial killer. Such a perfect getaway.

"I always told you that you were." He moved the invisible tendrils of my hair away from my forehead. My heart fluttered in excitement. Freedom...finallly! I was going to escape from it all. Finally, the accusations, the constant pain was going to end. I could go home, with Zayan. I could show everyone how I wasn't a complete failure.

This man...he had been so sweet and supportive. He used to annoy me so much, but no one had really put this much effort and trust in helping me. I felt grateful, quite in awe...a man clearly popular among women-so rich and powerful-was the only one who had trusted and helped me out of such a mess. Emotions struck me.

"Thank you." I shyly tugged on the grip on my hand, trying to hide my nervous ways.

"You are most welcome." His intense gaze stayed fixated on me, while I lowered my eyes due to all of the attention.

"Umm...you should stop acting so friendly to me now. We are so close to getting me out. This will start raising curious questions. U-Unless people are used to this behaviour of yours," I spoke awkwardly, stepping away from him. The last sentence had just slipped out. I hated how childish and insecure I suddenly sounded.

What the heck!

I didn't want to sound like one of those clingy wives.

I had no time for attachments and insecurities.

Triple Z had just been caught!!

"You are too innocent." Simply chuckling with amusement, Zayan pinched my cheek and smiled. Immediate embarrassment filled my veins. He had picked on my sudden feel of possessiveness and jealousy. Shoot!

"Whatever." I rolled my eyes, folding my arms to act nonchalant and unconcerned. Though, a smile stayed on my smile. I was super excited and couldn't wait for the next hearing. Yes!

"Women." He then shook his head in amusement and dragged one hand across his face with a mock show of exhaustion. "They have us acting like besotted fools and then still wonder about our loyalty. The audacity." He joked...a smirk appearing on his face. A blush appeared on my face.

This man was insane!

CHAPTER 15

1 st November 2019

Case: The Embalian Killing

Nyla

"The court, hereby, announces that Miss Nyla is non-guilty and should be paid 1000 rupees as compensation." The judge announced, causing a roar of applause to echo in the air. I couldn't believe it! I stood up in joy, shock and astonishment, clapping with joy.

We had done it!

My husband...he was a genius.

Zayan had proved my innocence to the world. In front of the jury, in front of the families of the victims...he had claimed that it was fairly possible that I had seen scavengers feasting over the bleeding victims of the Triple Killer and believed that it was the animals who hurt them. This was a convincing theory.

There wasn't really much to congratulate since lives had been lost, yet the air had turned lively and full of relief. People had got their closure. Families were shedding tears. I turned to look at them, and I could see many throwing me tender smiles. My innocence had been accepted. My family weren't in the country to see this, but I knew that hearing this would finally make them proud of me.

I couldn't wait to go and meet them!

Jumping up and down in my excitement with thrill and immense shock, I grinned widely at Zayan, eagerly waiting for him to do done with the formalities and watched in extreme awe as he received pats and hugs from the prosecution's team.

The whole atmosphere of the court had changed.

Many stood up to congratulate me. One woman sitting behind me asked me to marry the lawyer who had defended my case.

Everyone was super impressed by how Zayan had managed to help solve an incredibly complicated case. So many cards were being given to him, with many wishing for him to help them with their own issues.

This was our moment now.

Watching Zayan finally turn around and walk towards me, I met his confident and happy gaze, and my emotions...they just started spilling out. I began crying tears of joy and happiness. All my years of pain...I had been through a lot.

Yet, now, with Zayan by my side, the creatures were never going to torment me. The thought of living with no nightmares, no tensions and terrors...it made me feel so overwhelmed and almost in denial. The roar of the crowd seemed so far away in my own state of being shocked and being drowned in emotions.

Zayan finally reached me and pinched my wet cheek in adoration. I didn't know what to say to him. My emotions...they were just so high and triggered. I could only try to show him how grateful I was, and how hard it had been. I had been patient.

"I told you that I would take care of you." He tenderly patted away my emotional tears with his own shining with so much joy. "Now let's head out for a celebratory lunch."

"I would love to."

We had our lunch. The first official lunch as a couple in Zayan's favourite restaurant. He stated that now that the case had been solved, in a few days, he would officially have our marriage announced to the world.

Soon, after tasting some delicious dishes together and having Zayan's usual humour crack me up, we finally decided to head home.

It was nearly evening when Zayan had us driving down the empty streets of Embalia. He seemed so relaxed with on hand on the steering while and an elbow resting on the lowered window pane. Low poetry was playing on the radio.

I sat so happily, content and shy in his presence, with my hands folded. This day had been so awesome. This man-my husband-he was truly a gem.

"So are you going to brew me coffee when we head home?" I asked with a smile, reminding of him when he promised to do this for me.

"Actually, I have something to share with you." He turned to look at me, a rather pleasant expression on his face.

"What?" I asked, my eyebrows narrowing in confusion yet the smile still present on my face.

"I will be flying out tonight to meet my family." The relaxation in his voice, the hint of nervousness...it was a change.

"That is awesome!" I immediately grabbed his hand in support and joy. He was going to make amends. Just like I had told him. The thought of meeting his family made me feel a bit nervous, yet I knew that Zayan would be there to make sure I felt comfortable. And I would love to meet his family.

"I will drop you off at your parents' house and pick up up tomorrow afternoon. We will head out to our vacation home then." He started making plans, causing me to turn pale.

"Wait...I am not going with you? I l would l-love to meet your grandfather!" I tried my best to hid the panic out of my voice. This couldn't be. H-He couldn't leave me here. I had to stay by his side.

"You were right about me making amends with my family." He began rubbing the nape of his neck, completely oblivious to the raging storm inside of me. "I will make amends. My family is a bit different. We fight and sort out issues in a rather aggressive manner. I know there will be a lot of yelling. I don't you to hear that." He lightly chuckled, probably remembering some memory.

"Umm...it is okay. I can come with you. I won't mind." With sweat rising, I tried my best to hide my nerves and spoke in a nonchalant manner.

"I know. But, my dear wife...I won't dare let you feel uncomfortable. This is just till tomorrow. Don't worry. I will leave late at night after you are done looking at the clock in worry and fear. Also, I will bring grandpa along. He wasn't really talking to me before, but now...I am sure he and your dad would love to have lunch with us. And yes, I will miss you too." A knowing smirk appeared on my face, making me smile weakly in return too.

He thought it was just a matter of a few hours of the night. He didn't know that the creatures of my nightmares were night creatures. And they were waiting to hunt. My heartbeat started to pound first. Anxiety, suffocation, fear...all hit me hard.

I had to tell him!

The case had been solved, everything was in the clear. He had to know. I couldn't go back to my parents home. Again the creatures would attack, again the limelight...the creatures wouldn't spare me. They wouldn't. They wouldn't.

Lightly pulling away from Zayan's grip, I clutched the car seat with intensity and worked to build up some courage.

"Umm...Zayan...I-I can't be alone. There is something I want to tell you." I stuttered.

"What?" He frowned in concern, sharply turning his head in my direction, shocked by my abrupt change in mood. The look of concern, worry for me...it froze me for a second. This man had trusted me, defended my case. I couldn't tell him now that I knew who had killed those humans. I couldn't tell him how selfish I had been.

"I-I am afraid of the monsters in the dark." I tried with a different approach, wanting him to somehow understand. It sounded such a childish excuse, but it was the truth.

"Seriously?" He laughed, pinching my cheek. "My doe, once I am back, I will make sure they stay away." He was taking this as a joke. I did choose some childish words to explain.

"I am serious." I frowned, wanting him to hear my cry.

"I know, my doe." He finally caught on to my emotions and patted away the tendrils of my hair. "You don't need to worry about those anymore. I am here. All the pain you have been feeling, the tears you have shed...I know. I promise I will take care of you. I am actually making amends with my past because I want to start fresh with you. So, just for a little while...can you be strong for me?" He encouraged. I nodded in defeat.

"Umm...y-yes." I lowered my gaze, closing my eyes as he turned quiet for a minute.

"Good." This short and sincere reply broke my heart."

I will pick you up tomorrow afternoon. Also, I will call you at once I get there. Don't you dare switch off your phone."

"I won't." I nodded, standing before him, feeling so far away. My heart was beating so fast. He wasn't able to see the dread echoing in my soul. And I didn't allow him to see it. My heart was begging for him to stay, to not leave me behind, but how could I when him leaving had been a reality check for me. He would leave. He would go. These were my nightmares. Not his. As always, I had to fight on my own.

I couldn't tell my husband that I had been selfish. I couldn't risk sounding like a psycho girl, so I had to let it go. I had tried my best to make him understand, to hear my pain and fear. He didn't. Closing my eyes to control the tears falling out of my eyes, I breathed in as I had him catch one of my tears.

"Shh! Don't worry, Nyla. You are safe now. I will miss you too. And after this, I am never going anywhere with you. I had no idea that your pretty eyes would shed so many tears for me. Did I finally manage to win my wife's heart?" He smiled while cracking a joke, making me open my eyes and look at him with a weak smile,

"Maybe." Yet, my emotions stilled again because, from the corner of my eyes, I noticed the darkness, the movements.

They were here.

We were standing in my garden, and they had so cunning glided into my house. A sense of utter defeat and embrace of pain echoed in my heart. I could never escape. Never. He left with so many encouraging sweet words. I watched him drive away. My parents weren't at home. I was going to be all alone. The death of my best friend flashed in my mind. The creatures had been so brutal.

With a deep breath, I headed inside the house.

Zayan

Her emotions had been strange. From a woman who loved her distance, she had been quite eager to make him stay. There was a sense of emotion in her tone that made Zayan alert, yet the court winning had him determined into starting a new chapter with his wife. She seemed nervous. Too nervous.

He didn't want to leave his tiny little wife alone. But this whole experience had him acting with a rush of emotions. He wanted to spend the day obsessing over Nyla's eyes...just plain staring into them and listening to her hauntingly alluring tales...so this is why he purposely tried to listen without a tunnel view...

He no longer wanted the pain of the past to come between them.

Finally alone and feeling observant, he drove, with his mind racing to decipher all of her emotions. Clearly, she had been sharing half-truths, but he had stayed till the time she had stopped looking at the clock. Why was she still looking panicked? Was she simply missing him with the walls finally down? The thought made him smile. She was so cute and sweet. The way she mentioned being afraid of the monsters in the dark, it was oddly adorable. Yet a thought had struck him at such a confession.

Monsters in the dark...

A woman who had dealt with so much was scared of monsters in the dark. Zayan decided to swerve his car around and head to her place.

White lights, audience, monsters in the dark...

Something wasn't right. His heart felt at unease. There was a strange feeling of dread suddenly suffocating him. Maybe, he had been too impatient.

Upon reaching the house, he simply parked it on the ground and hurried out.

Loud shrieks of pain and torture were heard echoing in the air.

Oh, no!

Rushing inside the house in horror, Zayan screamed out his wife's name and watched in horror as he saw some strange creatures hovering around his badly wounded wife.

What the heck!

Zayan couldn't believe it. Was he dreaming?

His Nyla...she was shrieking and crying, as claws got dragged into her skin. These things...they were hurting her.

Watching her sink on the floor, sank his own heart in terror, and he immediately sprang in her direction...having his soul blanched with so much fear., worry and regret.

His Nyla...his woman...

She had tried to stop him!

The creatures stilled immediately as Zayan stomped in their direction. They seemed so sinister and malicious.

What were these things?

Suddenly, they began crying in shrilling voices and rushed away from him. Not even bothering with these measly things, Zayan sank down on his knees before Nyla and felt a horrified sob budding at the sight of his wife's condition. He was in complete shock.

Those eyes that filled his dreams were truly being his ruination.

His Nyla...she was so badly broken.

CHAPTER 16

N yla

I woke up with tears leaking from my eyes. The depression, the loneliness...there was no escape. My face, hands, cheeks were burning with pain. Scars, deep flesh-touching scars. Breathing in, I kept staring at the white ceiling of my room with extreme pain and defeat, holding whimpers of misery and despair, until a hand squeezed my resting hand.

"Sweetie, you are finally awake!" It was my mom. She was standing next to me, eyeing me with so much worry and pain.

"Ma..." Sob arose as I managed to turn my head in her direction. "It h-hurts."

"I will get your food and medicine." She immediately rushed out of the room, making me sob. So alone....so defeated and caged. I could never get away from these creatures. They would stay.

However, just as I was wallowing in self-pity, I heard loud and firm footsteps enter my room and head in my direction.

Zayan; looking so tired and dishevelled, he saw me awake and took large steps towards me.

"What the heck was that, Nyla?" His eyes were so wild, worried and concern. He grabbed my hand, running a thumb across my scars and stood hovering over me. I couldn't understand.

"I-I cut my-"

"Don't you dare lie!" His eyes blazed with fury as his jaw clenched. I had never seen him be this angry with me. My wounds were aching, and him screaming had me so overwhelmed.

Why was he screaming!

Why was he suddenly so angry with me!

He left. He was the one who left me again.

"I am not lying!" I yelled, sobbing as his tone hurt my soul. I had just woken up from so much pain, and this was what this man was choosing to say to me. Now of all times! Seriously!

"Then what was that I saw! What were these creatures!" He pressed his hands on the space next to me, leaning with so much tension. "Do you know what I went through when I saw you being feasted on some things around you! Look at yourself." He grabbed my hand again, which was covered in scars and wounds.

"What is this!" He was acting wild with emotions. I had picked on that my scars were hurting him too. I remember how horrified and fearful he had looked at my condition. I understood his anger.

"Y-You saw them." My voice turned low, as I lowered my gaze. I couldn't understand how he had managed to see. No one did.

"Yes." He pressed his hand deeper into the mattress. "Now tell me what were those things? Was it them committing the murders? Has it been them all this time? Was this your truth...the reason you were acting so terrified? Tell me why I had to see my wife getting tortured before my eyes!" His nostrils flared.

" Yes. It has been them," I spoke with guilt and shame, squeezing my eyes shut and fidgeting with my finger. My voice was filled with a sob...so cracky and pained.

"Why didn't you tell me?" He finally slumped down on the seat beside me, suddenly so tired and exhausted. "What is going on, Nyla?" He genuinely sounded so hurt and concerned for me. His concern hurt me more.

"I don't know, okay..." I opened my eyes and turned my head towards him. "No one saw them. I-I have been seeing these things since I was little, and no one believed me. I didn't want you to consider me insane, too. You didn't see these creatures at the forest, but today you did.

You are the second one to see these creatures. I have no idea why. They never showed themselves before. I have no idea what they are, but they are after m-me." I sobbed. My wounds hurting me bad. His stance finally softened at my condition, and he pulled his chair forward.

"Shh! Everything is going to be okay. Now I know..." He patted my hair in tenderness. "Nyla...when I saw you getting attacked... when I realized that I should have listened...you have no idea what that did you to me. My wife...you have no idea how much you mean to me."

"I didn't mean to make you worry. I-I-"

"I know." He interrupted, giving me a sad smile. "It was my fault. I was too impatient. I was selfish. But no more..." He assured. "I am going to inform the police about this. This is a discovery. Your family, everyone-"

"No." I quickly grabbed his hand, wincing as my wounds got twirled "You are to tell no one," I spoke with force. "They won't believe you. You will be labelled insane, too. No one is going to believe us. You are going to be quiet about this. Stay away from this mess. This is my battle. I will handle it. The creatures are scared of you. They won't do anything to you."

"What do you mean they are scared of me?" He frowned, narrowing his eyebrows in confusion. I looked away guilty.

"That day in the forest, the creatures rushed away in terror when they saw you. They were scared." I revealed, knowing the conclusion he would reach.

"Really?" There were so much shock and surprise in his voice. "Is that why you wanted me to stay by your side, is that why you said yes to giving me another chance?" The undeniable hurt in his tone pained me, too.

"That...and because you are the only person who has ever decided to protect me, adore me and be there for me. How could I ever say no to that...." I reached his gaze again in assurance, making him understand.

Both of us were in pain.

He leaned back in his seat and ruffled his hair. Momentary silence filled the air.

"Listen," He then grabbed my hand again, fingers running over my wounds. "We will get out of this."

"There is nothing-"

"Hush." He squeezed my hand. "I told you the northern areas of Pakistan, how people talk about mysterious creatures living there. We will go there. I know a man who is known for his knowledge and love of the land. He is old and wise. Villagers climb up to meet him at his home. I will take you there. We will find out what is happening. We will solve this."

"Okay." I finally nodded, my voice so tiny and vulnerable.

"Good. Now go to sleep. You need to get better before our journey. Beside...right now, your mom wants to show me off to your relatives." He joked, trying to lighten my mood.

I smiled, too.

Epilogue

Zayan

The evening sky was blazing. The mysteries of the world had astonished him.

What a plot twist!

Never in his life had Zayan dealt with such a mind-boggling case. So this was the reality behind the Embalian murders. He had no idea what those measly things were, and why on earth were they afraid of him. Why was his wife being targetted, and why was he such a dread for those creatures. Now their shrilling cries were making sense. When he had seen Nyla being attacked by those...the image was going to haunt him forever. He twirled his ring finger in an act of fumed possessiveness.

His!

No mysterious predator was going to take that away.

He understood why Nyla had kept it all from him. She was a labelled insane. She couldn't afford more rejection. He shook his head while thinking about just how over-confident he had been about his skills. This was the real mystery.

Standing with his arms folded behind his back, he closed his eyes and breathed in. The air suddenly seemed so vast and wild. So many mysteries in this world hidden in plain sight. The world seemed so huge and strange now.

He was standing on the balcony of the motel he and Nyla were staying at. They were finally on their way to Pakistan. Tomorrow morning, they were going to catch a flight to Pakistan, and from there, a new journey was going to begin.

Now no more secrets...he was going to solve this Embalian Killing Case, and this time...the woman holding his heart would share all her truths with him and allow him to be there. She was brewing some coffee for the night, claiming that she wanted to treat him for helping her, for forgiving her. It had made him smile.

Coffee sessions...that woman just knew how to have him act like a goner.

"Zayan," she finally called out to him. "Coffee is ready."

Sitting in the tiny lounge of their suite, Nyla was sitting so silently and formally on a sofa placed in one corner, while Zayan sat a table away from her, on a white couch. A dim yellow-lamp light was lighting the room. The atmosphere was so peaceful and relaxing.

The tray carrying the coffee cups was placed in the middle. Grabbing his coffee cup, Zayan leaned back and was in a mood to strike a lovely heart-to-heart conversation with his wife, tease her about being so formal and quiet, when he took the first sip of his coffee. An extreme sense of hurt, betrayal and misery hurt him hard. He wasn't really that shocked. All this time...he had sensed the edge of hidden secrets.

"Why?" He couldn't help but ask, taking another sip.

She had her eyes teary, yet there was a layer of coldness around her.

"I watched my best friend die." She spoke with an attitude. "I watched those creatures attack, and no one listened. I had to do something."

"I don't understand." He kept drinking, his soul bleeding with ache and misery.

"They wanted me, Zayan. I couldn't let them hurt me. So I made a deal; others instead of me. They listened. They are good at that. They are just so good at manipulation." Her voice raised with octaves, turned edgy and high-pitched.

"So all those people-"

"Yes," she nodded, sounding so bitter and alone. " I lied. I was luring those people. I was luring those people to the creatures; all those who hurt me. The creatures helped me manipulate, and then I lured. This was the deal. The moment they killed Nadia instead of me...I knew they had accepted my offer. They only needed preys. I got those for them."

"Oh, Nyla..." His voice was so full of disappointment.

"I don't want them to hurt me, Zayan. They will." She persisted, defending her choices. "They scare me so much. No one helped me. People only chose to hurt. I had to do something. There is no escape for me. I thought you could protect me, so I decided to stay by you instead of being used.

But now...after what happened, I know even you might not be able to save me. You have no solutions. You don't know the reasons. The man in the mountains might not be enough. So I have decided to once again deal with this on my own.

The creatures might listen to me again. They have expressed their anger. They will be in a better mood. If I manage to intrigue them by telling them about the place where people hold the knowledge of the mysteries living in the mountains, I can again make a deal with them." She spoke with so much hope and a hint of craziness.

"So Emir, Nadia...your college principal, Doctor Sana-"

"Yes. The creatures helped with the manipulation, and then I had the victims lured. I picked them. Emir was manipulated. The principal was spared by a minute, but he too was a slave of the mind." She accepted. She seemed so shaky, scared and broken. She was acting out. Zayan could see that. The sleeping portion he had been given was starting to sink in. He had tasted it the moment he took the first sip of his coffee, but the heartache was just too huge to make him stop drinking.

Yet another woman had turned out to be his ruination, just as he feared.

Droopy and feeling so exhausted, he closed his eyes.

"You made a b-blunder, N-Nyla. A-A huge blunder."

"It was me or them. I chose them." She shrugged.

Zayan lost consciousness before he could say anything else.

With him fallen asleep, Nyla felt her own heart bleeding out. He was a good man. Her husband...he had taken away her loneliness, been a breather in a world that shunned her, but she had battles that he would never be able to understand.

Her heart bled as she pictured life as a normal person. She would never have hurt this man. In fact, her marriage would have been the happiest day of her life. Closing her eyes, she pictured herself waiting every day for Zayan as a dutiful wife, cooking food for him, spending hours listening to his problems and making sure nothing hurt him.

Pain struck her as she thought of being his family, living in his vacation home, with the world applauding their happiness. But that couldn't be. The reality was that she had been one of the culprits of the Embalian Killings. She had fooled her husband. It hurt that things turned out this way between them, yet...she was just so scared.

The ideal home of hers had been crushed by her own hands.

She had been lying.

She had acted extra cold towards Zayan because she didn't want him to follow, to understand that she wasn't a good person. He had made a mistake by trusting her. It was time he went back home. This insanity...it was not meant for all. He had to stay away.

One 'labelled' outcast was enough.

Grabbing her purse from the sofa, Nyla got up and stretched her arms. She had to leave before the night. Walking up to her husband, she lightly patted his cheek and lowly whispered a sincere apology. His eyes did open a little at her words, yet he was too far gone.

"I-I will c-come for you." He mumbled.

Nyla could only offer a sad smile. It was a sleep-induced confession.

He wouldn't.

The wheels had shifted.

Nyla headed out, completely unaware of how her stubborn husband was not the one who lost. He was a man who won. She had managed to out-wit him. Well played!

Now it was his turn.

He would play the game of 'Chasing His Rose' and once he found her, he would show his wife the reason why even some mystic creatures were terrified of him.

He would act exactly like the infamous Detective of Asia.

Detective Zayan:

Witty, Smart and Ruthless-a deadly man with an iron fist.

So utterly bored...until provoked.